The Meaning *of* Children

The Meaning *of* Children

Beverly Akerman

Exile Editions

Publishers of singular
Fiction, Poetry, Translation, Nonfiction and Drama

2010

Akerman, Beverly, 1960-

The meaning of children / Beverly Akerman

ISBN 978-1-55096-148-5

I. Title.

PS8601.K47M43 2010 C813'.6 C2010-907180-8

Design and Composition by Digital ReproSet
Typeset in Baskerville and Lucida at the Moons of Jupiter Studios
Printed in Canada by Imprimerie Gauvin

The publisher would like to acknowledge the financial assistance of the Canada Council for the Arts and the Ontario Arts Council, which is an agency of the Government of Ontario.

Conseil des Arts du Canada
Canada Council for the Arts
ONTARIO ARTS COUNCIL
CONSEIL DES ARTS DE L'ONTARIO

Published by Exile Editions Ltd.
144483 Southgate Road 14 – GD
Holstein, Ontario, N0G 2A0

Canadian Sales Distribution:
McArthur & Company
c/o Harper Collins
1995 Markham Road
Toronto, ON M1B 5M8
toll free: 1 800 387 0117

U.S. Sales Distribution:
Independent Publishers Group
814 North Franklin Street
Chicago, IL 60610
www.ipgbook.com
toll free: 1 800 888 4741

For my family

The soul is healed by being with children.

—FYODOR DOSTOYEVSKY

BEGINNING

TUMBALALAIKA

When the arguing started, their voices would get louder and louder, till they broke into my dreams. That night, I woke and listened in the dark for what felt like a very long time. Perhaps I should have been afraid, but I wasn't. For one thing, they never yelled at Lisa or me, and for another, they argued so often I was used to it. Besides, I learned a lot when they fought. But that night, the uproar was exceptional. Even Lisa woke up after a while, and she stood there in the crib in her fuzzy footed pyjamas, fingers in mouth, her eyes shiny and round as marbles. I finally got out of bed and padded down the hallway to see what it was about this time.

The two of them stood facing each other in the small dining area, so close they could have spit at one another, leaning in, their faces angry and red. Together they made a shape like a deformed heart, broken at the bottom and lopsided because my mother was almost a foot shorter than my father. I watched as my father raised a hairy fist to his chin. He had been on the YMHA boxing team before they were married. "Keep it up, Andrea," he said, shaking his fist at her, "just you keep it up."

"What are you going to do, hit me?" my mother countered. She turned and pointed a finger in my direction. "Karen is standing right there."

My dad's head swivelled and we locked eyes for a second, then he hauled off and smashed his fist through the white wall beside them. There was a loud crash and, when he pulled his arm back, a round, dark hole. Frightened, I ran and jumped back into bed, telling Lisa she better do the same.

What shocked me most was that a wall could be so thin. I always imagined them rock-hard. Solid brick, all the way through.

So the next morning, when my father said we were going to Chomedey to see our new *house* and my mother said no, we were just going to look at the *flat* and they would make their decision later, I was pretty convinced that, no matter what she said, we would end up moving into that house or flat, whatever a "flat" was. My father usually made the decisions in our family, something that seemed natural to me then because he was so much larger and louder than my mother. He had black hair, not just on his head but all over, even on the backs of his hands. He had brown eyes and reddish sideburns. He let me stack his coins at the poker games he played on Saturday afternoons. My mother was pretty, even in anger, green-eyed with freckles and dark curly hair that she said had turned to straw since giving birth to Lisa and me. She wore black slacks and a royal blue cashmere sweater, her favourite, bought in those heady days before she quit working to be a stay-at-home mother. Those were the days, she would say, when she spent $100 on a pair of shoes without batting an eyelash. She was slowly ruining that sweater in the washing machine – she couldn't afford to dry clean it.

My mother was desperate to leave Montreal for the suburbs, where she said kids had the space to run around and make noise. She made it sound like so much fun, as though we would be yelling and roaring and banging on pots with wooden spoons all the time, like in *Where the Wild Things Are*. Until she made that comment about the noise, the thought of moving had left me feeling pretty desperate. My parents had taken the apartment on Cote St. Catherine Road when they were married. Of course, I thought it was perfect: it was the only home I'd ever known. Across the street was a big park, its swings set in the trees, like the middle of a forest, so you could swing in the cool shade instead of baking in the hot sun all the time. If you wanted the sun, there was the sandbox. The playground also had a series of twisting cement tubes, either end decorated with pieces of red wood suggestive of an engine and a caboose, so that together, the whole thing looked like a train. There was a wading pool, too, but my mother wouldn't let us use it. She said this was because she was afraid of water, because she had never learned to swim, but I thought she was also afraid of germs from other children, she just didn't want us to know. My mother was forever telling us how dangerous things were.

On the corner of our block stood an apartment building with two cement lions on either side of its three front steps. On our daily walks, Lisa and I would clamber all over the lions and whenever we did, my mother always stood right next to my sister, in case she fell. Lisa was a daredevil climber, part monkey, my mother often remarked. Once, we found her on top of a bookshelf as tall as my father. My mother said Lisa was too young to be afraid, that fear made you careful, that it was her job to be afraid for Lisa.

I also liked living around the corner from my grandparents. I visited them almost every day. My *Bubby* was very short, and she had orangey dyed hair, teased and combed and fastened on her head with hairspray, like a helmet. There was always ginger ale in her fridge and bright-coloured hard candies in a heavy crystal dish on the coffee table in the living room. My *Zaida*, also short, would always pick me up and hug me as soon as he saw me. "*Mamashayne*," he would say, and then he'd kiss one spot on my cheek three times – "muh, muh, muh!" He smoked a pipe, and he would let me smell the tobacco, sweet and scented with cherries, that he kept with him in a leather pouch. Both my grandparents spoke with thick Yiddish accents even though they had lived in Canada for over fifty years.

The street my grandparents lived on had recently had its name changed from Maplewood to Edouard Montpetit. My mother was convinced that the new name was part of a plot to erase all the English from Montreal. My father said, "Andrea," in that way he had – as though her name was really much longer – whenever she said something he didn't like.

According to my mother, we were moving because the apartment we lived in was getting too small. Sometimes she joked that the problem was that Lisa and I were getting too big. But I thought that the real reason we were moving was to get away from my grandparents. My mother was always saying they were too close, that they were too involved in her life.

Sometimes my parents argued about this, too. "My mother's so domineering, she's always trying to control me," my mother complained. "It's not enough that we come to her for *Shabbos* every Friday, but when we can't, she makes me send you over to pick up the food." My dad would counter by saying *Bubby* was just trying to do something nice for her, to help out so my mother would have less work, not have to make supper on Fridays – which was usually chicken soup, roast chicken, *lukshen kugel* and canned wax beans, with canned pears or homemade fruitcake for dessert – but my mother shook her head at that and said, "You don't know her. All my life she's been telling me what to do. You don't know what it costs me every time I have to take something from her."

Our car was a new black Pontiac Strato Chief with red seats and a shiny black steering wheel. There was a chrome Indian in a big headdress stuck on the door to the glove compartment, and a bobble-head Mountie travelled in the rear window. It was only May, and the Montreal heat was just gearing up, but the car was steaming inside from sitting for hours, all closed up, on the street in the sun. I rolled down my window and squinted through the hot breeze, searching for exotic licence plates from other provinces. Our licence plates used to say *La belle province*. Now they read *Je me souviens*.

"I remember what?" my mother asked, the first time she saw them. Then she answered her own question: "I remember how great it was here before the English came." I never understood why she was always so angry about this; we weren't even English. We were Jewish.

When my sister fell asleep in her car seat right away, instead of bothering me the whole ride the way she usually did, I decided that the trip out to Chomedey wouldn't be all bad. We drove down Decarie to Laurentian Boulevard, passing Canadair and a field that reminded me of the Emerald City from *The Wizard of Oz*. On the field, black men in the whitest short-sleeved shirts, long pants and shoes I had ever seen were playing a game my mother told me was called cricket. I thought that a babyish name for an adult game. My father said it was similar to baseball. Then there was about fifteen minutes of stopping and going, because the city was fixing the bridge. Chomedey wasn't on the same island as Montreal. To get there, we had to go over the back river. I wanted to know if there were any beaches we could swim at in Chomedey. My father said the water was too dirty to swim in. He pressed on the horn and announced, "In this province, there are only two seasons: winter and road work." Then he started to sing the way he always did in the car, his favourite Yiddish love song, "*Tumbala, tumbala, tumbalalaika…*"

After driving for almost an hour, we finally arrived, hot and sweaty, my legs sticking to the vinyl upholstery. I also felt a little sick; my father used to get carsick when he was young, too. I opened the door, hopped out, and threw myself down on the grass. This lawn didn't look anything like the shimmering green of the cricket field. Instead it was made of thick, sharp blades of grass, yellow dandelions, and cracked brown bald spaces. The sky was a light blue, edged with white. There was a very young tree, just planted, tied to a wooden stake. My mother told me it was put there to ensure the tree grew up straight.

"Sort of like a parent," I said.

She laughed. "Like a parent, except that that stick didn't make the tree. A seed did."

We looked up at the house. This kind of house was called a duplex, she said, two houses stuck together, one on top of the other.

"Which part's for us?" I asked.

"The upstairs," my father said.

"Maybe," said my mother.

"Andrea," he said, making her name sound very long.

I used my arm to shield my eyes from the sun and waited for my stomach to figure out we had stopped moving, a process that sometimes took a while. In the meantime, my father mounted the stairs and rang the bell of the bottom half of the duplex, and a moment later the landlord appeared. His name was Benny Laxer; he was a dentist and a friend of my uncle the accountant, the youngest of my dad's seven brothers and sisters and the only one who had gone to university. My mother's favourite sister had also gone to university, but partway through, my grandparents would no longer pay for it. So Auntie Sarah ended up at teachers' college instead. It had happened years ago but she was still angry at them. So was my mother, and not just for that.

My father never even made it to high school. He had quit school to help his parents make ends meet when he was twelve years old.

The two men shook hands and then came down the stairs so Benny Laxer could meet the rest of us. Benny Laxer was almost as tall as my father, but he resembled a basketball player more than a boxer. He had light brown hair and thick glasses and a son, my uncle had explained, who underwent regular operations to remove extra skin that grew between his fingers like webbing. When I heard about this, I had wondered if keeping that skin would have made him a better swimmer. Somehow I knew better than to ask Benny Laxer this as he greeted my mother, who held Lisa on her hip. My sister was still drowsy, slumped against my mother, fingers in her mouth, her head on our mom's shoulder. After a few more minutes, I got up, took my dad's hand and jiggled it until he bent over. I whispered in his ear that I felt better, and he patted my head.

"These girls been to the dentist recently?" Benny Laxer asked.

"No," said my mother.

"You should bring them to my office sometime, for a checkup. The little one go to sleep with a bottle?"

"No, never," my mother said.

"Do you live here?" I asked, looking up at him, one hand keeping the sun from my eyes.

Benny Laxer bent over, placing his hands on his knees. "No, honey, I don't live here. I live with my family in my own house about a mile away. I'm just here to show you the flat."

"What's so flat about it?"

"Hmm?"

"Karen," my dad ordered, "stop pestering Dr. Laxer."

The grownups didn't want to bother with Lisa and me any more than they had to while they took the measure of each other. My parents were trying to decide whether this was the right place for us; the suburbs closer to downtown, where my father worked, were nicer. Chomedey was the least expensive of the places they were considering, but it was also the farthest from the small factory where my father and his brothers made fur coats and hats. I had learned this and much more from eavesdropping during several of their arguments. Possibly Benny Laxer was trying to decide if we were the right people to rent to. He might have preferred a couple with no children: no dropping things down the toilet to see what would happen, no crayoning the walls, or swinging on the doors for fun, say. But who would move out here – “to the middle of nowhere,” my mother called it – unless it was “for the good of the children”? Benny Laxer knew our family. Because of this, he must have thought it likely that our rent would be paid on time, that we wouldn’t duck out in the middle of the night leaving the place a mess, like some of his previous tenants. That was why, according to my father, we were getting a good deal on the rent. My mother wasn’t so sure.

I knew where she would rather be: New York City, where Auntie Sarah, her “favourite sister,” lived. That was a joke, because Auntie Sarah was her only sister. They managed to stay close by speaking often, despite the long distance charges (another thing that could provoke angry words between my parents). Sometimes when they were on the phone, I would hear my mother say that she couldn’t understand how she ended up stuck in Montreal, married to this gorilla and with two little girls.

Auntie Sarah’s response, I imagined: “Shall I draw you a diagram?” This was one of their favourite expressions. One hot night the previous summer, when my aunt had returned to Montreal for a visit, the two of them had dragged kitchen chairs out onto the small balcony and killed a bottle of wine between them, repeating that expression to each other – “Shall I draw you a diagram?” or “Shall I paint you a picture?” Each time they said it, they would laugh till, as the night wore on, they were wiping their eyes.

Together we all went up the grey wooden porch stairs, and Benny Laxer unlocked the turquoise door – most of the duplexes on the street had their doors and balconies painted white or brown or turquoise – and led us inside. The staircase was steep and dark but, once we reached the top, it was very bright. The rooms looked large and airy; each had a wall of windows. The wood floors shone and the walls were a sparkling white. Benny Laxer said he had just had them plastered and painted. I spread my palms against them. They felt very cool and smooth, but when my mother caught sight of me, she hissed that I should keep my hands to myself. For the rest of our visit, I kept an eye out and only touched the walls when I was sure she wasn't looking.

There wasn't a curtain or a stick of furniture in the place. "When it's empty like this, it looks larger. It could be that, when we get all our furniture in, it'll be too crowded," my mother told my father. His face fell. I looked at her carefully. I couldn't believe she really felt this way. Had she said this just to make Benny Laxer think she didn't like the place? Was she trying to let my dad know who was boss? This was another thing they would argue about. Sometimes this discussion was called "who wears the pants in this family." I found this a bit of a mystery, because they both wore pants.

The bathroom had square white tiles framed by rectangular black ones, a white toilet and tub, and, on the wall with the sink, just above the mirror, a large thick, light fixture that looked like a giant throat lozenge. The walls were painted a deep, almost violent pink. In our apartment, all the rooms were white – this pink room took my breath away. I thought it was the most beautiful room I had ever seen. When I saw that bathroom, I immediately decided that my father was in the right on this one, but figured it would be smarter to keep my opinions to myself.

A door at the end of the kitchen opened onto a curvy black metal staircase, the kind of staircase that might lead to the dungeon in a fairytale castle. The metal slats of the steps had gaps between them. When I looked down through the gaps, I saw a small patch of lawn, the backyard, far below. For a second, I felt as though I was falling and I grabbed for the railing. It was the first time I realized I was afraid of heights.

Benny Laxer went ahead of us, and we all clanged down after him. My mother set Lisa down on the grass and Lisa immediately stood up and toddled over to the staircase where she started climbing back up, this time along the outside of the railing.

"You can use the yard anytime," Benny Laxer said. "I just planted that clematis by the fence and a lilac bush over there." He pointed.

My father turned to my mother, put a hand on her back and in a quiet voice said, "You love lilacs." She faced the tiny bush squatting in the shadow of the staircase, no more than a few twigs and leaves, really.

"Probably years before there'll be any flowers. Not enough sun," she said. Then she walked away from him to pluck Lisa off the stairs, saying, "Come back here, you."

As we were leaving, my father and Benny Laxer shook hands again. Benny Laxer said, "Better let me know soon if you're interested. I have a couple more families coming over this afternoon to take a look."

"We're going to see some other places, too. We'll think about it and let you know," my mother said. My father opened his mouth like a goldfish. Then he shut it again without saying anything.

I looked carefully the whole time but I never figured out what was so flat about the duplex. Only the walls and floors, far as I could see. But these were flat in our apartment, too.

The arguing started as soon as the car left the curb. "We have to let him know today," my dad said. "We should have told him we'd take it right then and there, left him a deposit before one of those other families do."

"Don't you fall for his malarkey. He's just trying to put the pressure on," my mother said. It escalated from there: Chomedey was too far, Saint Laurent almost as bad, Cote Saint Luc, which my mother had her heart set on, was too expensive, and we couldn't stay in Cote des Neiges because my mother was determined to get out from under the thumb of her own mother. My father kept insisting that the flat was perfect. Finally, he said, "Why don't we see what the kids think? Karen?"

"I liked it."

"Lisa?"

"She's three years old, Sam. Don't tell me you're going to let a three-year-old participate in this decision? And what about the neighbours downstairs?" She added, "You forgot to ask about them. What if they hate children, or have a big dog? Maybe they're the type who like to play loud music all night long."

"If you were worried about all that, why didn't you ask him? Why is everything always all my fault?"

"Who said that? I never said that."

"You never actually come out and say it, but you blame me for everything."

"I do not."

"Yes, you do."

"Well, I guess it's because you wear the pants in this family," my mother said.

My dad reached forward to snap on the radio and they didn't say another word to each other the rest of the way home.

That night, I dreamt the walls in our apartment were covered with dark holes. And as I watched, green and brown snakes poured out of them, wriggling their way down and along the floor, towards my bedroom. I ran ahead of them, my only possible escape out the bedroom window and onto a twisty black metal staircase. I was afraid to go out there but more afraid to stay, so I stepped through the open window – white curtains fluttering on either side – and rushed down the stairs. Suddenly, the staircase started rocking from side to side and changing shape, shooting up to the starry black sky one minute, rushing back down to the ground the next. I held tight to the railing with both hands and screamed in terror.

For once, it was my shouting that awakened my parents. My mother came to see what was wrong and, when I told her I'd had a nightmare, she took me back to their bed. My father returned to his snoring almost immediately. I lay there between them for a long time before I calmed down enough to go back to my own room.

Next morning, as usual, my dad had already left for work by the time I got up. My mother was pouring Frosted Flakes into a bowl when she announced that we were moving to Chomedey after all.

"To Benny Laxer's flat?" I asked.

"Uh-huh."

"What about the park?"

"There's a nice park named after John F. Kennedy that we can walk to," she said.

"Does it have a pool?"

"We'll get our own pool, set it up in the backyard, maybe invite some of the neighbours over." She poured the milk and put the bowl and a spoon on the table in front of me. "Eat, before it gets soggy."

"What about the neighbours? Do they have a big dog?"

"They have two daughters and a son, no dog. Dr. Laxer says they're very nice."

"Don't you fall for his malarkey," I said.

Quick as snake bite, she slapped my face. "You don't talk to me like that, young lady," she said.

My right cheek stung; I imagined her red handprint burned into it. I tried my hardest not to cry. I wouldn't give her the satisfaction. I put a spoonful of cereal in my mouth. It tasted like nothing.

Right beside me was the spot on the wall where the hole had been. The super had come and plastered it over, but that just covered it up. No matter how smooth the wall looked, I knew it was still there. I could feel it.

THE MYSTERIES

Like every other morning, this one starts with my mother's nagging: "Sit up straight, Rebecca. Don't talk back. Eat your eggs." But everything changes when she says, "Mark didn't sleep half the night and neither did I. It's probably another ear infection. We've got to leave now, before the line at the clinic gets too long. Be a good girl, Rebecca. Get yourself off to school for a change."

I say, "You're not driving me?"

"You aren't ready. And we've got to go."

"But why can't you drive me?"

"You haven't even started on your breakfast. You won't be ready for another fifteen minutes, Rebecca. And I told you, we've got to go now."

"But why can't you drive me?"

"You're not listening. Didn't I just say that Mark has to see the doctor? Then I've got to get to the pharmacy, get the prescription filled, and drop him off at the sitter's. And I can't be late for work today, I'm meeting a client. Rebecca, I don't have time to keep going over this."

"But you always drive me."

"Rebecca," she yells, "you're eight years old, you can get yourself to school once in a while!" She mutters something else, too. I think it's that I make her sick. She says that sometimes. Later, maybe she'll apologize. As if that makes it better.

"Fine," I say. But when she comes to give me a hug goodbye, I just sit there with my arms at my sides.

"Sack of potatoes," she says. "Be a good girl, and don't forget your key."

After they leave, I give up on breakfast. She always forgets to put cheese in my eggs. My dad never forgets. I wish he wasn't away so much, but what can you do, he says, it's a living.

For once, I put as much raspberry jam as I want on my toast. In the summer I pick raspberries up north. Raspberries grow like weeds in the country, that's what my grandpa used to say. Sometimes, when my dad's in a good mood, he'll make me jam from the berries I've picked. Even if it's only a little, enough for one small piece of toast or just one spoonful, he still makes it. It's special, something he does just for me.

I finish my toast, scrape my plate and leave the dishes in the sink. I pour my milk out, too. Because it's warm and there is nothing worse than that.

I find the things I need to put in my backpack: my lunch, notebooks, pencil case, and *Charlotte's Web*. I forgot. I was supposed to read some last night. I sit on the floor and flip to the drawings. My favourite is the one of Fern feeding baby Wilbur a bottle. Wish I had a pet. Not a pig, but

I'd take it if that was all I could get. What I really want is a dog. My mother says no way, you have to walk them and train them and they can get worms, she thinks that's disgusting. She says she doesn't have the energy to take care of one more living thing. I tell her I'd take care of it, but she doesn't believe me.

E.B. White. How'd he do that? Wish I could write a book. Then I remember I'm supposed to be getting myself off to school. I get my coat and hat, throw my scarf in the corner. I will say I forgot it. My boots are at the bottom of the stairs, I kicked them off when I came in yesterday. My socks get dirty with sand and salt as I walk down, my bag bumping along behind me. I hate that. Serves me right, my mother would say, is she supposed to bring my boots up the stairs too, she can't do everything. But why can't she, that's what I want to know? If I say that I'll get punished. Yesterday, she said she would call the police if I didn't behave, that the police take children away who don't behave. I don't want to believe her, but how do I know?

Outside, the streets are empty, nothing to see but duplexes painted white or brown or turquoise, each with a tree that stands like a dead stick out front. I go to check the time but I've forgotten my watch again. My mother makes a joke about me forgetting my head sometimes, but I never laugh when she makes it. Neither does she. Some joke.

She's supposed to drive me, she always drives me, but that's life, like my dad says. He also says no use crying over spilt milk, but it should be no use screaming over spilt milk.

Because I spilt some last week, and man, was there a whole lot of screaming.

The sky is grey with clouds that are dark and thick like long underwear after a day of tobogganing. Everywhere, the ice is fat, thick, and shiny. Water drips from the sides of the houses, snow melts from balconies. I can see my breath, but it isn't that cold, it's like the weather is deciding whether to stay winter or become spring. Then it starts to rain. My nose starts to run. I check my pockets – nothing. Finally, I wipe my nose on my mitten.

Halfway to school, only two more long blocks and now I'm on Elizabeth, the street where my school is. Up ahead, there's a man with a black umbrella, a long dark coat and bright-red earmuffs. He has grey hair, like a grandfather. My grandpa died last year. I miss him sometimes, we used to play checkers together. He was going to teach me chess. The man comes towards me and I go towards him. What should I say, because he is a stranger and I'm not supposed to talk to strangers, but he's looking at me and it would be rude to walk by him and not say anything, and I'm not supposed to be rude either, and why don't they tell you what to do about moments like this when they tell you so much other stuff, things that most of the time you couldn't care less about?

And then we meet. Because of the umbrella, he takes up the whole sidewalk, so I stop. His umbrella keeps the rain off me, we are that close. We look at each other. He smiles and says hello.

I say hello back.

"Nice day," he says.

I don't know what to say to that.

"Well," he says, looking around. "Not really. It's a day to be home drinking hot chocolate, isn't it?"

"Yes," I say, because he's exactly right. "With marshmallows."

His laugh is nice. "We can't have hot chocolate without marshmallows, now, can we?"

"No," I say. Imagine forgetting marshmallows if you're having hot chocolate. "And a fire in the fireplace, that would be nice, too," I say.

"Oh yes, a fire, that sounds good."

"And a puppy to curl up with. We could feed him marshmallows but not too many, because then he'd get worms. That would be disgusting."

"Lord no, that would be disgusting," he says and laughs again. "You're a real little character aren't you?"

I don't know what to say to that so I tell him, "I have to go. I'm late for school."

"Well, I'm going home now. I'll make some hot chocolate for us, light my fireplace, and think of you."

I thank him because it feels like the right thing. And then I wish I could go with him, be someone else's child. My throat gets tight. I could have a puppy and some adventures, maybe write a book about it when I'm older.

"You go to that school up there?" The man points with his head.

"Yes. Just up the hill."

"Not far now. You won't be too late," he says. And I can tell he's a really nice man. I feel tears in my eyes. Silly, just because someone is a bit like your dead grandpa and nice to you when you're late for school and your jacket's getting wet right through and your mother only thinks about the baby and not enough sleep and that your father is never home and isn't it his baby too?

"I'm going now. Enjoy your hot chocolate."

The man is still smiling. "Pleasure meeting you," he says. He touches my shoulder as I pass. I have to hurry, it's very late, I can tell.

At the school, light shines like gold from the windows. It looks so friendly. How come I never noticed this before?

Inside, the halls are empty. I'm later than I've ever been. What will Mrs. Spence say? She's the nicest grade two teacher but still. I put my things in my locker and my feet in my running shoes and think about the corner. I've never been in the corner. Maybe this will be my first time. I will hate it, it will be so embarrassing. The door is heavy, the brass knob shines. Mrs. Spence stands in front of the class, her long red hair tied back today. Behind her is the blackboard, already full of writing, and above that, the alphabet in cursive. On the wall is a picture of the Queen wearing her crown. Mrs. Spence looks at me, everyone does. I feel hot, I feel embarrassed. Then I'm crying. I run to Mrs. Spence, and she puts an arm around me as I press my face to her scratchy brown skirt.

"Here, here, Rebecca," she says. "What's all this, then?"

I can't say anything. She smells like clean laundry. And chalk dust.

"Class, please take out your readers and start the next story, 'The Naughty Squirrel.' I'm taking Rebecca out in the hall for a moment." She takes my bag off my back and leaves it on the floor, grabbing some tissues from the box on her desk as we pass it. We go out the door and sit on the bench. She hands me the tissues and I blow my nose.

She says, "Goodness, what's wrong Rebecca? You're so late today."

I look at the floor, black and red, like a checkerboard. I swing my feet. "My brother was sick, my mother had to take him to the doctor, and she couldn't wait for me, so I walked to school myself. And I was afraid you would put me in the corner." I try not to hiccup.

"Oh, Rebecca. Please don't worry about the corner. Sometimes things happen and we're late and that's okay. So long as we're doing our best, the people who care about us understand, okay? Right, Rebecca?"

I nod. I can't look at her. What she says is nice but my best isn't always enough. She pats my back. I'm afraid that if I look at her, I'll cry again.

"Are you sure that's all this is about? Because you've been late before, Rebecca, but you've never come in quite like this."

She's so nice. There has to be a reason I'm so late, doesn't there? "A man stopped me on the way to school," I tell her.

She moves her long red ponytail off her shoulder. "A man," she says. "On the way to school." She sits quietly for a bit, then adds, "Was it someone you know?"

"No," I say, "it was a strange man."

"Did he talk to you?"

"Yes."

"What about?"

"Hot chocolate."

"Hot chocolate," she says. Her voice changes but I don't know why. Is she mad? Because I stopped to talk to him? She's being so nice to me and now I'm making her mad?

"Did this man ask you to come with him for hot chocolate?"

"He talked about hot chocolate and the weather. He said he'd light the fireplace at his house. He asked if this was my school."

"Did he talk about anything else?"

"Puppies. I'm not allowed to have a puppy." Now why did I tell her that? It just jumped out. What I don't tell her is that once, my parents sat me down and told me we were going to have a new addition to the family. I thought they meant a puppy but it turned out it was just the baby coming.

"We should go to the office," Mrs. Spence says.

I shake my head.

She says, "Rebecca, sweetie, please don't cry. It'll be all right."

I nod and blow my nose.

The vice-principal walks by and Mrs. Spence calls out, "Miss Harding, could you take my class while I bring Rebecca to the office?"

"Of course," Miss Harding says, coming over to us. Miss Harding is very tall and thin. She stares at Mrs. Spence for a moment, then at me. Did Mrs. Spence say something? If she did, I didn't hear it. Maybe she just moved her lips, but why would she do that?

We walk to the office, Mrs. Spence holding my hand. The lights hum, her shoes click. This isn't good. I feel a pain in my stomach.

At the office, Mrs. Spence speaks to the secretary, but I can't hear a word she says because my heart is thumping so loud in my ears. The principal's office is worse than the corner. Only the worst-behaved children are sent here. The pain in my stomach gets stronger.

Mr. Norman is bald and wears a blue suit and tie. He smoothes the tie over his belly and tells us to sit down. His office is huge and white. On the wall, there's a big clock with black numbers and red hands. We sit down. Rain slides like pearls down the windows.

Mrs. Spence says, "Rebecca met a strange man outside the school on her way in this morning and it's upset her. Isn't that right, Rebecca?" The smile leaves Mr. Norman's face.

I nod, all of a sudden remembering my father telling me his teachers used to smack his hands with a ruler when he misbehaved. And then my grandpa saying, "That's nothing, we used to get the strap across our buttocks." I swallow hard. Maybe I shouldn't have said anything about that man.

Mr. Norman tells me to stand outside the door. The secretary has frizzy brown hair and a puffy face. Her fingers whiz along the keys. I watch her, wishing I had a typewriter.

When they call me back, Mr. Norman's on the phone.

Mrs. Spence says he's calling the police. "Maybe they can find the man before he talks to someone else."

I bite the inside of my cheek. "Why the police?" I say. "I hardly spoke to him."

"Because he may be dangerous," Mrs. Spence says, and this is big news to me. How do grownups know these things? I wish I knew. I guess that's why we go to school. Not just to learn math and French and spelling and gym but for other things. For mysteries.

"Can I… may I please have my mother with me if I have to talk to the police?"

"Of course," she says, "but you mustn't be afraid, because the police are here to help us." That's the kind of thing they tell you at school. She doesn't know how many times my grandpa said that the police are a bunch of damn crooks, no better than the gangsters.

When Mr. Norman gets off the phone, Mrs. Spence asks him to call my mother.

"No, wait," I say, "maybe she can't come. It's tax time."

Mr. Norman looks at Mrs. Spence.

"Rebecca's mother's an accountant," she says.

I don't want my mother to come. She said she'd call the police if I kept misbehaving. Now the police are coming. Maybe she'll tell them to take me while they're here, because she gives up. She says this sometimes when I make her angry, when I take things from the baby. Or spill the milk. She says I make her sick or push her round the bend. Like she hates me. She never says these things about Mark, not even if he keeps her up half the night. Now I'm crying again and I don't even care anymore if they see.

The secretary gets my mother's work number from a file cabinet. Mrs. Spence hands me more tissues and pats my back. Mr. Norman calls but my mother isn't there yet, so he leaves a message, asking her to call him. The police arrive and, man, are they tall and they wear such dark jackets and hats. My stomach feels bad again. Mr. Norman and the secretary bring in more chairs, but then Mrs. Spence decides to return to class. When she leaves, it's just me and the three men. The police tell me their names but I'm so scared, I forget them right away. The older one has a big grey moustache, you almost can't see his lips when he speaks. The younger one looks like a high schooler, he still has pimples. The police put their jackets on the back of the chairs and their hats on the principal's desk. Their hats are speckled with shining beads of water. Their guns are on their belts, in brown leather holsters.

That's when I know the police really are big trouble, just like grandpa said.

"I had a little girl like you," says the older police. The way he says it makes me want to ask what happened to her. Maybe she would know better than to talk to strangers if her father's the police.

"Should we wait for her mother?" says Mr. Norman.

"We better not, we might lose him," says the police. He turns to me. "Do you mind answering a few questions?"

I nod.

"This man who spoke to you, what did he look like?"

"He was an old man, even older than you, like a grandfather," I say. "He had grey hair and red earmuffs."

"What else was he wearing?"

I tell them about the long dark coat and the black umbrella.

"Colour of his eyes?"

"I don't remember."

The policeman isn't happy. "He have a moustache or a beard?"

"No," I say.

"He tell you to come with him?"

"Not exactly."

"Either he did or he didn't," the policeman says.

"He talked to you about hot chocolate, right?" says Mr. Norman. "And puppies?" Both policemen look at him, then back at me.

"Did he tell you to come with him?" the policeman asks again.

He told me he'd light the fireplace for me, didn't he? "Yes," I say, "yes, he told me to come with him." My stomach takes a bit of a dip.

"Did he touch you?"

"He put his hand on my shoulder when I walked by."

"Was he trying to keep you from going?" asks the older policeman.

My stomach dips again. Why would the man do that? And why is the younger policeman here, anyway? He never says anything. "I don't know," I answer.

"Either he was or he wasn't," the policeman says again. He's starting to sound mean.

I think about this. He touched my shoulder. To keep me from leaving? Why else? "Yes," I say then. "But I ran away from him, to the school."

"He asked if this was your school, right?" says the talking policeman.

"Yes."

"Did he say he'd come back for you?"

This scares me, too. Why would he come back? "I don't remember."

"Either he did or he didn't," the policeman says, and now I'm sure he's mad at me. "Maybe," I say.

"Maybe's not an answer," he says. He sounds like my mother when she says I make her sick.

"Why would he come back for me?" I turn to Mr. Norman. He doesn't say anything, just puts his hand up to tug at the knot in his tie.

The policeman asks again, "Did he say he'd come back for you?"

They're all making me mad now. Why doesn't Mr. Norman help? And why did that stupid man start talking to me, anyway? This is all his fault. I stick out my chin. "He said he'd come back," I say, and suddenly my heart is jumping in my chest. Because this is a big, fat lie. That man better not come back. If he does, they'll put him in jail, and it will be all my fault. And when they find out I'm lying, I'll get into real trouble. I think about the ruler and the strap. They don't do that anymore, do they? I start feeling like I might throw up.

"Right," the policeman says. He stands and turns to Mr. Norman. "We'll go on out, see if we can find him. He can't have gotten far." Then he turns back to me and says, "You shouldn't talk to strangers, missy. Didn't anybody ever tell you that?"

And that's when I stop looking at him. I can't say anything else. This is all my fault, I know it. I should have been on time. If I hadn't dawdled, I never would have met that man, never would have spoken to him.

"Well," he says, and then the other men stand up, too. The policemen put on their stuff. Mr. Norman shakes their hands, thanks them for coming. The young one still hasn't said a word, but he ruffles my hair as he walks past me, the older one, too. My grandpa used to do that, instead of a hug, he said. But why would the police want to hug me?

When they're gone, Mr. Norman takes me back to class. He pats my head as I pass through the classroom door. I go sit at my desk.

"All right?" asks Mrs. Spence.

Mr. Norman nods and leaves.

I look at the corner, try to smile, and say, "Yes, all right." My voice is funny.

"Good," she says. "We're looking at page 87 in our math book."

So I go up to her desk for my backpack, then back to my seat. I get out my books and pencils but I can't do any work. The numbers dance along the page. That's too bad, because math is usually my favourite. It's still raining. I pick at a scab near my elbow till it bleeds. I don't look at anyone. I feel funny about the crying and everything.

At 11:30 the bell rings but before I can pull out my lunch, Miss Harding is at the door saying my mother is at the office. When I think of the police, my stomach feels bad again.

I leave all my things. "You can get them later," Miss Harding says. She doesn't give me her hand. Mrs. Spence watches us leave with a funny look on her face. I wonder what it means. Worried, maybe? That makes me feel worse.

In the hallway, there are hundreds of kids talking and walking and running, pushing and teasing until they see Miss Harding, then they stop. But as soon as we pass, I know they'll start up again and she knows it too. So how come I'm the only one in trouble?

Miss Harding's legs are so long, I have to rush to keep up. We get to the quieter part of the building where the principal's office is. Miss Harding has an office here too. It's smaller of course. Because she is the vice-principal and he is the boss of the whole school.

I look up and at the end of the hallway I see my mother in her camel hair coat with the large buttons, leather gloves in one hand, her purse hanging over her arm. Behind her, light spills from the windows in the school's front doors. She looks very beautiful, her lips the colour of raspberry jam. She stands talking with Mr. Norman. She is taller than him and much, much younger. He tries to stand straighter, what a silly thing. We get closer. I start thinking maybe I should turn around and run back down the hall because she will surely have had enough, she will give up, I will really have made her sick this time.

Miss Harding says, "Rebecca, dear, let's get a move on."

My mother and Mr. Norman stop talking then and turn. No one says anything, we just stand there and look at each other.

Then my mother drops her purse and gloves and walks towards me. Her heels click, the lights buzz. The pain in my stomach spreads till even my heart hurts. She comes right up to me, stops, and stares down. I have to look up at her. I want to look away but I can't. It's like this moment is frozen, like this moment is deciding whether to stay winter or become spring. Then she drops to her knees and throws her arms around me, hugs me so tight, it takes my breath away. "Honey, oh honey," she says, "are you really okay?" Her next words all run together. "Tell-me-baby-sweet-Jesus-are-you-really-all-right?"

And I am so surprised. I was sure she would yell at me. She will when she finds out. Lying is much worse than talking to strangers. And lying to the police, sending someone to jail… I can't even bear to think about how bad that is.

Over my mother's shoulder I see Miss Harding with her hand on her mouth. Mr. Norman clears his throat and looks away. My mother keeps holding me. Hard. I hug her back hard, too. The pain fills my whole inside. I close my eyes and try to think of good things, like raspberries and my grandpa and puppies, and my dad coming home soon. But then I see the police in their black uniforms, the gangsters and the guns, the ruler and the strap. I think about all the things I don't understand, like how do they know that that man was dangerous? Why did he talk to me? What will happen when they find him? And how come I told all those lies?

And I know I can never ask. Because if I do, everyone will know how bad I really am. And because I'm only eight years old, and grownups never want to explain anything.

BROKEN

When you're a kid, one of the things you understand best is that about most things, you understand almost nothing at all. But by the start of my eleventh summer, one thing I *had* figured out was that when people lowered their voices, it was usually because they were talking about sex. I first made this association because of Audrey, who lived two doors over with her parents and her two little sisters, all of them strawberry blondes. Her sisters were so cute – Amy, two years old, and Alice, almost one. "Irish twins," my mother called them – which was weird, because they went to synagogue with us, and I knew for a fact that no one in their family had ever set even one foot in Ireland.

Every night after supper, the kids of my neighbourhood gathered to play hide-and-seek, and on one of those nights Audrey and I slipped into the honeysuckle bushes, both of us twitching and slapping because of the mosquitoes, doing our best to defend ourselves without making too much noise. The sky deepening like a bruise, Audrey turned to me and whispered, "Last night, my mother told my father she's going to wear panties to bed every night. To prevent any more accidents." Fireflies flashed around us in some sort of secret code.

I didn't want Audrey thinking I was stupid, but around my house an "accident" was whenever my sister Lisa woke up with her bed wet. I was sure, though, that Audrey meant something else. It was the look in her eye. "Accidents" weren't exactly covered in Art Linkletter's *Where Did You Come From*, a record my mother had given me and my sister in the spring when she told us she was pregnant. Just about the time she stopped working. Just about the time she started being mad at everyone, all the time.

My mother was afraid of dogs so I'd given up wishing for one, but if I could have had a dog, I'd have chosen one just like Lady. She belonged to the Applebaums, who lived just across the street. The size, shape, and colouring of a Dalmatian – same spots, same whip-like tail – Lady's hair was longer and feathery, like a collie's. Happy and excitable, she sometimes danced around like those Lipizzaner horses featured on *The Ed Sullivan Show*. She'd run in circles when she saw me and come whenever I called, even if the Applebaums told her not to.

That spring, Lady got pregnant just before she was supposed to be "fixed." Mr. Applebaum was furious – he used to leave Lady in the backyard on a leash attached to the clothesline. On the other side of the fence lived a small brown dog named Digger, and Mr. Applebaum was forever shouting at the kids who owned Digger whenever the little dog made his way under the fence. Digger's adult owners were so incensed by the shouting that once, they'd even called the police.

When I first found out Lady had to be fixed, I felt funny. I couldn't stop thinking about it, but I just couldn't bear to ask my mother to explain it. I finally decided it could mean only one thing: that until someone patched them up, girl dogs were somehow broken.

By the time school finished, Lady's puppies were expected any day. With humans, my mother said, this was called "giving birth," but with dogs, it was called "whelping." Well, whatever it was called, for a while it was all anyone talked about, the puppies and how they were made. For most of us, this marked our first experience of S-E-X. At my age, boys were a trial, but they clearly possessed some vital knowledge that we girls lacked. They whispered stories none of us completely understood, from the vaguely unsettling to the downright horrifying, like the one that ended with a boy pissing in a girl's face. Gradually, the impression formed that, at least for girls, sex was like that wave in *The Poseidon Adventure* – something huge and scary, dangerous and getting closer all the time.

That movie gave me nightmares for months.

In the fullness of time, Lady whelped her six puppies and that was when it hit the fan at the Applebaum house: the grownups had only expected two or three. That night after supper – my mother having said "No, you can't have a puppy," at least a million times – she was scraping spaghetti into the garbage and stacking the dishes when my dad said, "Now aren't you glad you're only having the one?"

For an instant, my mother froze. A noodle slithered from the plate she held and glopped to the kitchen floor. She turned that look on him, the one my dad called the evil eye, and said, "You think this is all a big joke, don't you?"

"Come on, Andrea. You're just upset about losing your figure again. And about those varicose veins."

"I'm upset because I had to quit working."

"The doctor said you need to rest more, anyway."

"The doctor said—" she took a deep, angry breath. "Funny how men get to make all the decisions, how you have all the fun—"

"Not all the fun."

"—and the women get stuck with the consequences." She sounded mad enough to spit. "Maybe I should've had you fixed."

My dad's face got very red as my mother stamped over to the sink with the dishes. He looked at Lisa and me, cupped a hand to his mouth, and said in an almost-whisper, "That's just the hormones talking."

"I heard that," my mother said.

We were all quiet, Lisa and me sipping our juice, Dad staring at the ceiling. Dishes and cutlery clanked under running water.

After a while, my dad cleared his throat. "What's for dessert, honey?"

And my mother answered with something really weird: "Sorry, chief. The bun's in the oven but it won't be ready for quite a while yet."

Adam was my downstairs neighbour, tall and skinny, his hair, eyes, and freckles the same orange-brown colour. He was forty-three days older than me, and proud of every second of it, as though it was something he himself had had a hand in. We couldn't have been more different. For one thing, Adam had a rude mouth. And he couldn't sit still – or stand still, according to his mother – so he was always in trouble at school. This embarrassed his mother, a grade three teacher at our school. She had hoped to make it to vice-principal once-upon-a-time, a hope that went down the toilet, she'd told my mother, when Adam started kindergarten and let the world know he was a problem child. Adam had both a chemistry set and a dissection kit. He was always making stink bombs out of ballpoint pens and cutting open earthworms or any other living thing he could get his hands on – mice, tadpoles, even a grasshopper once. By contrast, I was a teacher's pet, with dark hair and eyes and an extra ten pounds on me. The excess weight clung to my hips and chest, and left me with the secret feeling I was nearly a grown-up woman.

One lazy Saturday, a few days after the puppies arrived, my parents went out with Lisa, leaving me to hang around at Adam's. We decided to head for the park. It was too hot for me to enjoy the swings – in the full sun, the movement made me queasy – so I sat and watched Adam swing as high as he could and then jump off with a whoop. We climbed on the monkey bars and later, chased each other around, ending up in the hedge maze atop the hill in the middle of the park. It was cooler there – there were a few small stuccoed alcoves we could duck into and hide in, but they often reeked of urine, or occasionally, something even worse. We found one that wasn't too bad and slumped down with our backs against the wall, panting, as our eyes grew accustomed to the gloom.

"I'm bored," Adam announced. "You want to play doctor, Karen?" He leaned over and pulled open the neckline of my t-shirt, saying, "Let's give a listen to your heart, shall we?" He sounded just like our pediatrician.

I slapped his hand away, hot all over. "Stop it, you idiot!"

"I'm just kidding around. Anyway, what's the big deal? It's not like you've got something to hide," Adam said.

"You big, fat idiot."

"Takes one to know one."

I hit him again, harder this time, then took off, out of the maze, down the hill, and across the field till I ran out of steam near the sandbox. I plopped down beside a bunch of toys someone had left behind – a pail and shovel, some old wooden spoons, a hand-powered eggbeater that suggested the *Starship Enterprise*, and a big old yellow dump truck.

Adam straggled over and folded his gangly legs in the sand beside me. I turned away to poke around in the grit.

"What're you doing?" he asked.

"Nothing."

He picked up a wooden spoon and started digging. "I saw this show about these terracotta warriors they found in China," he said, like it was a question. He went on – how the statues had been found by farmers drilling a well, what terracotta was composed of, how the warriors had been made thousands of years ago in one place and assembled somewhere else, hundreds of them, with chariots and horses, that they had all been buried beside some old emperor.

I wouldn't look at him, just kept digging, first with the shovel, then with my hands, until my fingernails were stuffed so tightly with sand that they hurt. "We better go back," I said.

"Let's go see the bitch's puppies," he said.

"A grownup hears you talk like that, you'll get your mouth washed out with soap."

Adam looked from side to side, eyes wide, shoulders hunched, chewing on the fingers of his right hand. "Oooh… You see any grownups hanging around?"

"I'm just saying."

"Let's get going, okay?"

We brushed the sand from our backsides and raced toward home, Adam in the lead, me puffing a little behind.

I stopped several times to pull my shorts out of my bum crack. My shoes had filled with sand. I'd have to sit down eventually and fix that, too.

The Applebaums lived in a duplex. Shorecrest was a street of duplexes. But it wasn't near any shore I knew about. When I asked questions about such things, my mother would sigh and tell me to run out and play. Then she'd light another cigarette.

Sandy Applebaum came to the door, an eight-year-old, blue-eyed headful of black curls. "Come through the garage – my parents are mad about all the kids in the house but they keep hoping you'll get your parents to take a puppy."

"I wish," I said.

"We're thinking about it," Adam said, which was news to me.

We trooped down to wait by the garage door, Adam snapping his fingers, then making fart sounds under his arm. He pulled a super ball from his pocket and began bouncing it. "Maybe we can play Stand-O later," he said.

"We'd need more people."

"I know that, stupid."

"I'm just saying."

It was cool and shaded, the smell of cut grass and damp clay in the air. It had rained the night before. "Maybe it'll be another summer like last year, when it only rains at night," I said.

Adam, still bouncing, answered, "That'd be neat." He pegged the ball at me but I jumped away just in time.

As soon as the garage door was open a couple of feet, Adam and I scrambled beneath it.

Adam stopped bouncing and gave a low whistle, then reached out and fiddled with a lock of my hair. I swatted his hand. He turned to Sandy. "The puppies open their eyes yet?"

"Nah, it's too soon. And keep it down, okay? My parents are taking a nap."

"A nap? It isn't even lunchtime," Adam said. He got this big, stupid look on his face.

I poked him in the shoulder. "Quit it."

He said, "Quit it yourself," shoving me against Mr. Applebaum's workbench. We made the short walk in silence, Adam again bouncing his ball, me rubbing my arm.

The basement was made of concrete, cool and dark; the smell of dog mingled with musty earth. Sandy flicked the switch on a bulb that hung from the ceiling like a luminescent spider. Lady lifted her head and looked at us, shifting her tail slightly. I put my hand to her nose. She pulled away and lay back on her side in the basket. Beneath her was a red and black plaid blanket. My dad kept one just like it in the trunk of the car for picnics. The puppies mewed and scrabbled over each other.

"They sound almost like kittens," I said, the three of us squatting beside the basket. "Aren't they cute?"

"Aren't they *key-ute*?" Adam imitated me. "You sound like *such* a girl."

"I am a girl." I reached out to touch the wriggling bodies. Two black, two black and white, one white.

"Where's the brown one?" Adam asked, like a mind-reader.

"I don't know," Sandy said.

"Oh, come on, what did it do, run away? They don't even have their eyes open yet."

Sandy brushed her curls out of her eyes "Lady wouldn't let it nurse. She kept pushing it away. My mom stayed up all last night, trying to feed it warm milk. She tried a doll bottle, the finger of a glove, even an eyedropper. Nothing worked."

"So where'd it go?"

"I don't know," Sandy repeated, her forehead wrinkling. "My dad said there must've been something wrong with it, or Lady wouldn't have kept pushing it away like that."

I tried to imagine it, a mother refusing to feed her baby. This was a Jewish neighbourhood: the mothers I knew practically force-fed their kids.

"It must be dead," Adam decided. "Maybe if we dissect it, we can figure out what went wrong."

Sandy and I looked at each other.

Adam said, "You know tomcats'll kill their babies if they get the chance? Then the mother cat goes into heat again." He smiled a big ugly smile, moving his eyebrows up and down.

"Don't be gross," I told him.

"Maybe your dad flushed it down the toilet."

Sandy yelped, "No way!"

"The toilet's for fish," I said. "A puppy's too big for the toilet."

Adam narrowed his eyes at me. "Bet it's in the garbage, then."

"My dad would never!" Sandy wiped the back of her hand under her nose and sniffled.

Adam turned to Sandy. "He'd have let you watch if he buried it. He'd have asked if you wanted to have a funeral or something. So he must've thrown it out. Where's your garbage?"

I glared at Adam. I wanted to kill him.

Sandy said, "In the garage, but *don't*—" but Adam was already gone.

We streaked after him. Daylight flooded under the half-open door. Adam had already dragged the aluminium cans nearer the light and removed their lids. One was empty; he pawed around in the other.

"Stop that!" I yelled, and I put my arm around Sandy, who sniffed and swiped at her eyes.

"God, this stinks," Adam said.

It was true. The smell was overwhelming. And though I'd been told over and over that Jews weren't supposed to pray for anything specific – like getting a perfect score on a math test or a new bike for your birthday – right that second, I prayed my hardest that that puppy was miles away from where we stood.

I went to Adam and put a hand on his arm. He looked at me and I jerked my head toward Sandy. He glanced her way and shook my hand off. A moment later, he said, "Screw this," and banged down the lid, slapping his hands on the back of his shorts. "Let's go hold them."

We marched back to the furnace room and sat down. Lady raised her head again at our approach, and slowly settled. When I put my hand towards her this time, she just moved her head away. I could hardly believe this was the dog who had jumped around me, mad with happiness, only weeks before.

Each of us picked up a puppy, their eyes shut as though sealed with crazy glue. I chose a black and white one, the one most like Lady, and lifted it to my cheek. It felt like the velvet dresses my sister and I always wore for the high holidays. Its heart throbbed against my hand. "Wish I could have one," I said. Sandy laughed, a puppy squirming in the crook between her neck and shoulder.

When Adam's puppy let out a squeal, Lady lifted her head and whined, sniffing the air. "I didn't do anything," he said.

"Yeah, right." I looked over and said, "Don't hold it like that, you're hurting its back."

Adam turned the puppy on its stomach. "Just wanted to see what it is. It's a girl, poor thing."

"Fuh-nny." I put my puppy back in the basket and Lady began nuzzling and grooming it, her tongue moving in long, rhythmic strokes.

"Wow," Adam said, "take a look at those titties!"

That was when I noticed Lady's nipples – huge, strange, stretched out things, the rubbery red of a hot water bottle. Adam reached forward and tugged one. Lady yelped and sat up, growling, her teeth bared. I'd never seen her like this in all the time I'd known her.

"You hurt her," Sandy whispered, her cheeks pinking up, her eyes glassy.

Milk began oozing from the nipple, a small stream that puddled and soaked into the blanket. Lady turned and sniffed it, and then began licking at herself. The puppies scattered, squealing.

"Oh, that's disgusting," Adam said. "*She's* disgusting."

And suddenly I was standing, hands clenched, my heart hammering.

"Karen?" Adam said.

Sandy looked up at me, too.

A wave of heat surged through me. "You… you stupid fucking fucker!" I shouted. "She is not disgusting!"

For a moment, nobody moved or said a word. Even the puppies were silent.

I turned and ran on shaky legs, through the dark garage, under the door, into the blinding light of the afternoon. I raced across the street, rushing home, but then I remembered that no one was there and kept on going. Down the block, around the corner, onto Notre Dame, the bigger, busier street. Sand swished in my shoes, uncomfortable, but I couldn't stop. I even turned my ankle once, a sharp jabbing pain, but I kept on. I ran as though something was chasing me, my heart a wild thing trying to burst from my chest. There was only one thought in my head: I had to find my mother. There was something I needed to ask her, something very important.

I just wished I had the faintest idea what it could be.

POUR UN INSTANT

Our friends, vacationing in Israel for the month, had given us the run of their cottage in the Laurentian mountains, north of Montreal. And it had been one of *those* trips up, the kids squawking with the regularity of a metronome: "Sascha's looking at me." "Kara *pushed* me." "He's on my side!" "Am not!"

David glanced over at me, smiled his wry lopsided grin, mouthed the words, "Natural birth control," and held my hand for the last fifteen minutes of the ride.

But now that we were finally here, car unpacked, kids in the water, cool Chardonnay cradled in a wineglass, my body cradled in the Muskoka chair, I remembered why we'd come. There was something about being quiet beside a large body of water. Usually I couldn't stand it, this feeling of being at the edge of eternity. But it wasn't so bad here, on a smaller lake, some place where the possibilities were not so open-ended.

It was August but so long as we stayed in the sun, warm enough. In the shade, the air held the merest hint of alpine bite, more like a tender nibble. David puttered, a ladder propped against the side of the blue clapboard cottage from which he reconnoitered the eavestroughing. This was how he relaxed, playing Mr. Fix-It. Anything to do with ladders made me tense, but they do say opposites attract.

The sun, the kids laughing and splashing, the small sailboat in the distance, the pines like dark sentinels on the far side of the lake… I was happy. I drowsed in the chair, looking out over the water. My eyes slid out of focus; it was as though the rippled waves were strewn with stars.

It was the summer of '73 and I was fourteen. I remember the day I first stood on the grainy sands of Wasaga Beach. Georgian Bay's cobalt expanse of trapped hydrogen and oxygen confronted me. I'd discovered that fact – that water was actually composed of two gases – in science class the previous year. Things weren't always what they seemed, and they could change in an instant – super cooled ice could morph into vapour. Sublimation, they called it. I wondered how far such laws went. Did they apply only to things, or to people, too?

We'd come from Montreal to visit the boy we'd fostered for three years, vacationing in Wasaga with his extended family. A shaft of sunlight, cued by Cecil B. DeMille, pushed through the towering cumulus clouds that floated above the water. I imagined heavenly background music, could almost see Charlton Heston descending Mount Sinai, his hair and beard newly white. My toes squinched wet sand, forming grooves that filled, gradually, with water. It was summer's down slope. School would be starting in a few weeks and I couldn't afford to waste another minute. I shouted for my sister to join me and threw myself into the water.

Later, looking back at the beach, I saw my mother on her folding lounge chair. She was reading a magazine, probably her favourite, the *Ladies Home Journal*. They had this feature she loved: 'Can this marriage be saved?' I'd started reading it too, eventually realizing that, according to the magazine, every marriage was worth saving – though it took me a few months to catch on. Reading was basically what Mom did at the beach. She refused to go in the water, afraid of it because of stories her father had told her when she was growing up. *Zaida* had seen a cousin drown, pulled into the vortex of some roiling river in Bessarabia. The old country. I was impatient with this perennial excuse of Mom's for avoiding the water but, to be honest, I was always impatient with her. In my heart, I could never quite credit a grownup being afraid of anything. To me, they all still seemed equally omnipotent.

I was a chubby kid in a red bathing suit with a little white skirt that fluttered at my hips. The suit had a navy and white striped insert between my breasts, or what passed for them, anyway. Earlier that summer, after buying it at Woolworth's, I cut the soft virginal cups away because their empty flopping felt like a reproach. But I'd also accidentally cut a sliver of the suit itself and when my father saw what I'd done, he'd bellowed. The walls must have shaken because, in a domino effect, the table hockey game that was propped up against the living room wall toppled over. At the time, my guinea pig Dickens, black with a white stripe girdling his thick middle, was waddling about, and the falling hockey game – forever Habs versus Leafs – crushed and killed him. It was a potent demonstration of another of those unwritten laws, the one about unintended consequences.

Everyone still thought of me as a child, but there was something in the backbeat of my heart, propelling me toward puberty, that demarcation line, that no-woman's land, with a relentless, at times giddy, exhilaration. It was like lying on the train tracks in that moment just after you were certain a train was coming. My little eggcup breasts had nipples that still dimpled inwards. The merest downy quiff of hair dusted the mound between my legs. I was still a girl, but I was in restless anticipation of those experiences I knew were just, tantalizingly, out of reach.

I discovered an interesting new use for the electric toothbrush that summer, and spent inordinate amounts of time in the bathroom – the only room in our house with a lock – supposedly in pursuit of dental hygiene. The idea came from the section on vibrators in a book my mother let me read: David Reuben's *Everything You Ever Wanted to Know About Sex (But Were Afraid to Ask)*, quite a slim volume, considering.

The Baron de Hirsch Institute had placed Akiva in our home; my mother always called the social services organization "the Agency," as though referring to a higher power. Akiva's Romanian parents were embroiled in a divorce and going through some really tough times; the words "nervous breakdown" flitted like hummingbirds between my parents and the social worker. Even then, I knew Akiva for what he was, a stand-in for the baby my mom lost before I was born. Although it had happened almost twenty years earlier, she would still cry if the subject came up.

Akiva had left our family some months earlier, just when things were getting interesting. According to my dad, we were there "to see how he was doing." Somehow, my parents evolved this peculiar travel strategy: we'd never go anywhere unless a family visit justified the trip, like a flesh-pot of gold at the end of a rainbow. Perhaps they were Jews fed up with wandering. As near as I could figure, family was what they lived for and of course to a kid, this was the epitome of boring, the acme of uncool. Nonetheless, every summer, we'd meet up with cousins in Ottawa or Dad's maiden aunt in Toronto. Once, we drove all the way to Niagara Falls for a reunion of the North American Hitzigs. There was a wax museum full of macabre exhibits – mostly set pieces of gruesome murders past – and also a place where you could get your picture taken in a mock-up of a barrel going over the falls. The jewel in the entertainment crown was a small amusement park, the kind that probably sported a questionable safety record. Coloured lights beamed onto the falls at night. During the day, we peered over the wrought-iron guardrail that separated us from the Falls, and watched the *Maid of the Mist* – a tour boat – get buffeted by the torrents of water sluicing over the cliff in an endless, monstrous roar, a staticky sound, like the threat of chaos. We never took the boat ride ourselves:

Dad and I suffered from motion sickness. And predictably, my parents deemed it too dangerous.

Was the Holocaust the source of this Jewish penchant for risk avoidance, just one more symptom of our collective posttraumatic stress disorder? Maybe it was older than that, atavistic. Maybe we'd been that way ever since the destruction of the Temple in Jerusalem and our march into exile, thousands of years before. Disaster-poised.

My sister and I splashed about, playing tag in waist-high water. When I next glanced over at my mom, Akiva was there. But he wasn't dressed for swimming. Instead, he was decked out in beige chinos and a white shirt, the sleeves rolled halfway to his elbows. Below his shirttails, limp with heat, dangled the fringes of his *tzitzis*, the prayer garment he now always wore beneath his clothes. I knew he'd become observant since moving back with his father but this was the first I'd seen of it.

I called out to him, arms windmilling, legs churning the water in my haste to get up there, to be with him again. I noticed he had a *yarmulke* on his head, too.

"Hey, Marce, look at you! I hardly recognized you, you've grown so much," was his greeting as I wrapped myself in a towel. I didn't like that much; it made me sound like a kid. I was unsettled. I wanted to hug him but I was soaking. And besides, he'd taken a step back when I'd gotten to shore. It was awkward, suddenly. I felt shy. Things had changed.

He and Mom continued speaking as Lori and I devoured the chicken salad sandwiches and ginger ale we'd brought down to the beach. We crowned the feast with twisted ropes of red liquorice. When Akiva was ready to go, I volunteered to walk him off the beach. We were only a few blocks from the group of houses that the community had rented that summer. Orthodox Jews, they always travelled in packs. In fact, if you stood before their dwelling places and narrowed your eyes just the right way, you could almost make out the flapping tents and, nearby, the camels, squinting into the sun, waiting patiently to be formed once again into caravans and make their rock 'n' roll way across the ancient, almost-unremembered world.

"'Member last year, when we went to Mount Royal?" Akiva said to me as we walked along.

"Yeah." As if I could forget. Akiva had taken me to the Harmonium concert last year, on the June 24th holiday. *St. Jean Baptist. Le Saint Jean. La fête nationale.* The Quebec we lived in in the '70s – I could hardly call it *our* Quebec – was a frothing cauldron. We lived through the awakening of the *maîtres chez nous,* the burgeoning nationalist movement, people who self-pityingly called themselves "the white niggers of North America." There were mailbox bombings, kidnappings and even several murders, including one of a government minister. It was our version of the '60s convulsions. A bit late, sure, but that's the way it always was in Quebec. Maybe it was a question of translation, the time it took for ideas to permeate geographic or linguistic barriers. Our neighbourhoods weren't quite burning (after all, we were *Canadian*), but our communities, schools, and institutions were doubly segregated, not so much by race as by language and religion.

The concert on Mount Royal had been our little secret. We went all right, for the music and the adventure, but we kept our voices down, at least at first. Once we settled in, however, we quickly let go of our apprehensions, holding hands, surrounded by – merging with – all the others, singing, dancing, feeling that shiver of the forbidden as fireworks spangled the summer's dark. *Pour Un Instant.* For a moment. I heard again the dulcet harmonies, about running out of time to find enough time. About having to discover our own stories, our own lives. It had been magical, heavenly, the happiest, most perfect night of my life. But a girl couldn't help but hope for more.

I shook the memories away and asked Akiva about life with his dad. I knew his mother was still in an institution. It didn't sound like she'd be getting out any time soon.

"It's different, you know? Not bad, just different. My dad though, he's really, really happy. He's got it all planned. When I finish high school, we're moving to New York. I'm going to university there."

"You lucky duck! I'd give *anything* to get to New York."

"Yeah, sure, it'll be a blast." Akiva sounded like he needed some convincing.

"Well, I think it'd be *great.* I just don't get it, why we can't go. It would be so exciting, don't you think, to drive down, maybe even fly? All those museums and shows.

They're building, like, the *tallest* building in the world there, the World Trade Center. And then there's Coney Island, the United Nations, the Statue of Liberty, the Rockettes." My grandparents had provided me with this wealth of detail. They went to New York every September, just before the holidays. That was where they'd bought me my first miniskirt, orange with white stripes. It came with a sweater – white with orange stripes – and a shiny white belt. I'd wanted that miniskirt so badly, the ache was almost physical.

"Your dad's worried about the crime rate."

"Not *that* again." Always looking for an excuse to touch him, I poked his shoulder. He felt solid, warm. Real. "Maybe if you're there, they'll change their minds, eh?" Akiva *and* New York: it was more than I could have hoped to cram into one thought.

We reached the sidewalk and said our goodbyes. Lori, Mom and I left the beach soon after to shower, change, and make our way to the house that was hosting that evening's *Shabbos* dinner celebration, to see how we could help. There must have been twenty people rushing about, half of them children. An orgy of silver polishing was taking place. We could smell the *challah* baking, and something with cinnamon, an apple cake maybe. Preparations were ongoing for the *cholent*, a gargantuan pot of stewed meat and beans that would cook all night on a low heat and be served for lunch the next day.

That evening, Lori ran a fever and my parents decided to go back to the motel early. Akiva volunteered to walk me over later; we'd been warned there were some rough kids round town at night, that it wasn't safe to walk alone.

It was after ten when I was ready to leave; the candles had burnt themselves into darkness. There was still a lot of talking and laughing going on, singing even, though the littlest ones were starting to droop.

Outside, heat shimmered, rising finally like a prayer. It was warm but not too humid, a perfect late-summer night. We walked, the streetlights few and far between, and in the anonymous darkness I took Akiva's hand. He didn't even glance at me but for a heartbeat, he abandoned a monologue about his extended family living in Brooklyn. He kept hold of my hand though, and then began talking again, as if nothing had happened. His grip was warm, sure and dry. I could feel the calluses left by his schoolbag.

A swarm of teenagers came up from behind and pushed their way past us. One guy looked back and, with a smirk, flung a few coins our way. His friends sniggered while Akiva and I froze, pennies bouncing around us like hail. Then the boys melted into the shadows. Occasionally, we would catch sight of them up ahead, faces lit by flickering matches, hilarity punctuated by bottles clinking in brown paper bags.

"Want to walk along the beach?"

"Sure," I said, "why not?"

We changed direction, by unspoken accord putting as much distance as possible between ourselves and the other teenagers. I slipped my sandals off and felt cool sand caress my feet. Slate-coloured clouds smudged the pristine moon;

there was the lightest possible breeze. We ambled to the water's edge, staring out over the sparkling vastness. It appeared large enough to cover the whole world. At that moment, it was hard to tell where my hopes ended and the sky began.

Akiva escorted me to the motel each of the few remaining nights of our visit. All we did was hold hands and talk; still, it was good to be together. He confided in me and I felt wonderfully grown up. Akiva told me that his new life felt like a plunge into cold water. He hadn't made any close friends yet and found his new world hemmed in by too many expectations. Even though he was grateful to be reunited with his dad, he felt very sad about his mom, and because he felt that some essential part of him was withering away. Was he supposed to simply turn his back on everything he'd looked forward to? Drinking, dating, girls, sex? If so, he was finding it hard. Despite his dad's happiness, the promise of his previous life still hung over Akiva like a cloud.

"Thanks for listening, Marcy," he told me one night, his tone, even to someone my age, unbearably earnest.

I studied him then, the dirty blond curls and pleasant familiar features, the wide cheekbones. I sensed more than saw the weight he'd recently gained and the height, the way his body was deepening into adulthood. Waves shushed and summer's lushness scented the breeze: freshly mown grass, greasy french fries, the tang of wood smoke from a bonfire somewhere down the beach. "No big deal," I told him. "It's been my pleasure. Anyway, I've missed you."

"Yeah," he said, turning away but taking my hand again. "I've missed you, too."

And then it was over; my family was preparing to leave for home the next morning. That night, I suggested a final walk along the beach.

"Sure," he said, "why not?"

I'd taken to dressing like the religious girls: full-skirted seersucker shirtwaists that tied in the back. I couldn't have said why; it was a case, I guess, of "when in Rome." A chill in the air raised goosebumps as it whispered against my bare legs, and I shivered.

We made our way past the dunes and, on a whim, decided to try out the lifeguard chair. Neither of us had been up there before and it seemed like the perfect time to try something new. The glimmering lake filled the entire horizon. I asked Akiva to put his arm around me, telling him it was for warmth.

"You're cold?" he asked, glancing down at me.

I nodded back, suddenly tongue-tied as I gazed up into his face. Then we were kissing, our mouths jumping the distance between us like magnets finally aligned just so. I felt glittery as the constellations, and wouldn't have been surprised to see sparks shoot from my fingertips. Parts of me I couldn't even name were making their tingling selves known. We lay back against wood worn smooth by generations of sandy bottoms.

And then there were voices below and a flashlight splashed over us, like a bucket of ice cubes.

"Hey, John," a disembodied male voice called out, "someone's up there. Hey you!" he shouted up at us. "It's time to come on *down*," the last word elongated, like the announcer on a Bob Barker show.

We complied quickly, guiltily.

"Well, well," he said after a brief lick of silence, "a Jew boy and a Jew girl. I didn't think you kids were allowed to get up to this kind of thing."

My gut clenched.

"Aw, c'mon Tim, leave 'em alone," his companion protested.

"What are you, a fucken Walton now? Eh, *John-Boy*? It's not enough they run the rest of the world, these rich bastards? They have to come up here, too, push us aside, shove their superior ways down our throats? *The chosen people*. And we're just s'posed to smile and take it all?" The light wavered; liquid sloshed in a bottle as he took a hard swig.

"Tim, get off it now. Let's just go someplace else."

I could feel Akiva next to me, shocked into stillness. We stood there blinking in the light, like fugitives recaptured.

"How 'bout I invite them to a little party, Johnny-boy? What do you say to that, you two? Want to have a little *partay*?"

"No thanks." Akiva's voice sounded stronger than I expected. "I'll just walk my friend home now." He turned to me, turned to go. A hand shot out and grabbed his forearm. The flashlight shook. Light splattered over us like rain.

"No way, Jew boy. I'll tell you when you can go."

"What the fuck're you doin', Tim? Let 'em go, eh? You don't even know them. What've they ever done to you?"

"Shut up, John-Boy. Just *shut* the *fuck* up."

"Okay, that's it, man, that's the *limit*, man. I've had enough of your crazy shit. I am out of here." And John-Boy crunched his way across the sand, a man of abandoned principle.

It was quiet for a moment; the waves lapped, oblivious.

"Take your clothes off."

"No." Akiva spoke for us both.

"I *said* take them off."

"I don't think so," Akiva answered, his voice smooth as milk.

There was the sort of click a Zippo might make and then the thin tongue of a knife was catching the moonlight.

Akiva turned to look at me then. "I'm sorry," he said. I started to cry, quietly as I could.

We stripped down to our underwear. Akiva stood in his *tzitzis* and y-fronts. I wrapped my arms tight around myself, shaking in flowered bikini panties and my new flesh-coloured bra that snapped closed in front.

"Take 'em off, take 'em off, take 'em *aaall* off," our tormentor chanted.

"No," Akiva told him easily, putting a hand on my shoulder, steadying me. "This far, no further. You're drunk," he went on in a measured tone, "you don't mean any of this." But the Force wasn't with him.

"You *SHIT*," the young punk roared, "I'LL tell YOU what I mean!" Akiva pushed me hard then, towards the street. The flashlight fell to the sand and I ran for my life, chased by the grunts and groans rising behind me.

I woke with a start, sweeping my wineglass to the dock. The crystalline sound of it made me think of the broken glass that concludes Jewish wedding ceremonies, a symbol of the destruction of the ancient Temple in Jerusalem, recalling us to tragedy even in the midst of celebration. But this wasn't a wedding; the glass simply landed on its side and rolled, the liquid dribbling away between weathered grey boards, staining the wood with enlarging darkness. In it, I could still see the blood pooled black in the sand, the slash through Akiva's prayer garment, the alabaster lips marking the gash into his liver.

That night, David built a fire in the pit by the small, sandy beach. We all doused ourselves in bug juice, hunted for whip-like sticks that would double as skewers and feasted on roasted marshmallows till we all agreed we felt like a bunch of Michelin Men. I'd found a battered guitar in the back of a closet. I tuned it as well as I could; it had been a long time since I'd last played. We sang together, familiar folk tunes I'd always sung with the kids – "Leaving on a Jet Plane," "Michael, Row the Boat Ashore," "If I Had a Hammer." I told the twins how happy I was they were getting along so well and they wriggled, faces shining in the firelight.

"Now, you'll have to bear with me 'cause I'm going to play you a song I haven't heard for a really long time, and you two," I said to the kids, "you've probably never heard it before. You won't know all the words but you're in French immersion: you should understand some of it. Someday, I'll explain it all to you, but for now, just listen, okay?" I looked over at David. I wanted desperately to touch his mussed-up hair, the Wedgwood blue sweatshirt stretched across his large, warm chest, the pleasant familiarity of his wide cheekbones and full lips, all of him. He made my heart leap in my chest like a silvered trout.

I was surprised at first, how easily it all came back: the chords, the feeling of the instrument in my arms. I started to sing, finally. *Un Musicien Parmi Tant d'Autres*. The lyrics were yearnings, for days and people gone by, for a time when musicians had real stories to share. A twelve string elegy for those we had brought into the world. For those to whom we should listen.

I began to cry, as if I would never stop. David came over and tried to take the guitar away, to put his arms round me, but I wouldn't let him. So instead he scooped the twins into his broad embrace.

"Mum's okay, guys. She's just feeling sad; we all get sad sometimes. Anyway, it's past your bedtime," he told them, matter-of-factly. I watched him, little heads tucked onto his shoulders as they made their way back up to the cottage and the comfort of their beds. I remained down by the fire, staring into the pit for hours.

When all the wood was exhausted, when all that was left were the dying embers, flickering orange glow-worms, I got up and went to the edge of the dock. The water undulated before me in the moonlight. I closed my eyes and saw again that ghastly tableau, the scaffolding of all my nightmares. I stood there, as though balanced on the cold edge of eternity, feeling the pain of things that change forever, of love that could turn to death in only an instant.

I don't know whether I jumped into the water then or if I fell, but suddenly, I was in the shock of its cold embrace. I slipped down, down, down into the darkness, until I felt such a pain in my chest, I couldn't tell if it was my lungs bursting or my heart breaking. But the pain galvanized me, and I thrashed my way to the surface, popping back up into the night air, sputtering and crying.

Then I set off for the other side of the lake, relieved and yet destroyed to find myself still in love, and still, ferociously, alive.

MIDDLE

LIKE JEREMY IRONS

In the waiting room, you avoid catching anyone's eye. At least, that's the strategy you set out with, an automatic sort of etiquette. To look down at your lap for a while, till you feel comfortable enough to look about and discreetly trawl for stories more sordid than your own. It's very close quarters here at the General. No longer OB – only GYN, the maternity ward closed ten, maybe even twenty years ago, Montreal's English community's closing up shop. The department only performs gynecological surgeries and abortions now. Abortion slots fill up quickly, allotted, like all operating time, to affiliated doctors with admitting privileges.

First, you called the clinic to ask them what to do. They gave you the names of a few private practice doctors. By the time you finally decided and called the clinic back, your "procedure" was scheduled two weeks later than the date you were first offered. The price of uncertainty: two week's peace of mind.

Usually, you shop around carefully before condescending to see a new doctor, but this time you go to the first gynecologist who would have you, who has time available.

Usually, you refuse to see a male doctor (you hate having male doctors!) but this time, you found yourself lying there, legs spread-eagled, assuming the most immodest pose on God's green earth. He examined you, to corroborate your story. The speculum snapped open, the sound of a small skull being wrenched from its spine. The examination done, he told you to get dressed. Afterwards, you sat on a chair, glad for the expanse of desk between the two of you. And then you came to, to the realization that he was grilling you, that by law you were required to convince him of the medical necessity of the "termination." You paused. It was a necessity, all right, but a *medical* necessity? That's like when the emergency crew shocks your heart to get it beating again, isn't it? To bring you back to life?

An abortion would be just like that.

The waiting room is small, windowless, and beige. The fluorescent light casts its wave/particle glare on the posters that line the walls: gruesome venereal diseases, nagging about AIDS. By 10:00 a.m. the chairs are almost filled, the room crammed with women's bodies, their sweet exhalations and murmurs suggestive of piety, of nuns at prayer.

The loudest people in the room are a pasty trio of students in their early twenties. From the university next door, you guess. The young man and woman stand, courage bolsterers for their friend who, seated, is the protagonist of this dramedy. He has dark, wavy short-cropped hair, black sideburns, and those thick black-framed glasses that, at some point when you weren't paying attention, morphed from nerdy to cool. Definitely not the father. The other cheerleader is in black jeans and a nubby charcoal sweater shot through with jewel-coloured threads. As she chatters, she keeps pulling her sleeves down over her hands. The woman they are there to support is chalk-pale, her wispy black hair caught in a loose chignon. She smiles repeatedly, tremulously. They share quiet laughter that hangs on a few beats too long, carrying within it a quality close to hysteria. Been dumped, you think. Or a one-night stand. Date rape, maybe?

Across from you sits a slim black woman, about thirty or so. She looks like a churchgoer. Her belted brown shirtwaist dress bears a small pattern of white, pink, and turquoise. She wears no makeup, her hair tied neatly back, slim ankles tucked under her chair, black shoes with chunky mid-sized heels. Her hands are neatly clasped around a small format magazine, what you take to be *Reader's Digest* or a romance. No, you decide, she'd hardly be reading romance today. This place was anathema to romance. Here's a list you'll never see: abortion clinic pickup lines:

"Come here often?"

"First trimester or second?"

"So, how many weeks along are you, anyway?"

"What's a nice girl like you doing in a place like this?"

You imagine that you are all asking yourselves this last one, anyway.

You already have two kids. Girls, one four years old, the other eighteen months. The little one has the chubbiest legs, you call them thunder-thighs. She's just starting to talk, putting words together like beads on a string. The older one is serious, very serious. She asks questions constantly, trying to understand everything: where the sun goes at night, how mosquitoes make that buzzy sound, where babies come from, why mommy's crying again.

Of the big decision, your husband said, "It's your body." Perfectly, politically, correct. But you feel his sadness like the throb of a second heartbeat.

The difference between planned and unplanned? It's the difference between tropics and desert, consensus and rejection, love and rape. You are colonized by a foreign power, an alien's tentacles extending deep inside your true centre. It has taken five long weeks for you to decide that, at this time and in this place, the latter is your truth.

The first time you got pregnant, you knew almost immediately. Your period was two days overdue. You already had an appointment scheduled with your GP, you were having a check-up in advance of you and your husband's first big trip together. The two of you were about to travel to the motherlands, England and France.

"I think I may be pregnant," you told the doctor.

"You were trying?"

"Yes, actually."

"For how long?"

"Three months or so."

"How many periods have you missed?"

"I haven't missed any yet. I'm only a couple of days late."

She raised her eyebrows, her eyes widened, she tilted her head to one side.

You held your ground. "I just have this feeling,"

"What kind of feeling?"

"You know the way a cat kneads a pillow before curling up on it? I feel like my uterus is doing that." You opened and closed your fingers for her, made a sort of squeezing motion.

She held your gaze a little longer than strictly necessary. You wanted to tell her that you have always been extremely simpatico with that part of yourself, the hidden inside. You know when you ovulate, aching for a day or two, one side each month, alternating. There is no other explanation for these pains, they've gone on for years and years. Maybe every woman is capable of knowing so long as she hasn't been chemically neutered. You have often wondered why women would saturate themselves with chemicals for decades just to be sexually available for a few hours a week. It seemed illogical and beneath your dignity, so you have always refused birth control pills.

Now, here in this waiting room, you wonder if dignity has its price.

The doctor handed you a johnny coat and pulled the curtain closed, triggering a sound like wind chimes. You stripped. You're always careful to fold your underwear neatly and this circumstance was no exception. Once on your back, you hitched your lower half down to the end of the examination table. The paper liner beneath crackled in protest. The doctor helped your heels find their purchase and examined you, taking the opportunity to scrape out a Pap smear.

"Well," she conceded, feeling around, post-speculum, pressing hard inside and out, "it's *poss*ible that you're a few weeks pregnant." She still sounds dubious. "We start counting from the first day of your last period. We'll do a blood test for pregnancy hormones, it's more sensitive than the urine test. The hospital lab will have the results tomorrow. I'll call you."

"It's just that we're going away, you know? We'd like to know for sure so that we can tell our families before we go."

"Sure," she said. "You can put your clothes back on."

Later, after all her prodding and pushing, you realized you could no longer detect that cat-kneading feeling. You worried she'd killed it. But she hadn't.

A middle-aged couple sit quietly, side by side. Once in a while, as though he's just remembered, he takes hold of her hand. But they are the exception: most of the women here sit alone, unspeaking. Their eyes look inward and far away. They seem to be in meditation.

The receptionist calls you in one at a time, every fifteen minutes or so. And unlike any other clinic you have ever been to, here they only call out first names.

It's your turn. The nurse hands you a hospital gown, a pair of slipper socks for your bare feet, and a couple of capsules to take with the tepid water she has provided in a small waxed paper cup. You swallow them down, wonder how your throat can feel so dry with water in it. You search out a place to throw the cup that you hold, crumpled, in your sweaty palm.

Then, as the pills begin to take effect – Valium and some other muscle relaxant, things you've never taken before – she sits you down, has you sign some papers and talks to you about "the post-procedure protocol." If you move your head too fast, the room spins. Everything in it seems to shimmer. The nurse's words become hard to make out. It's like you're doing fifty in a hundred-mile zone.

"You'll probably have to wear sanitary pads for the next four weeks or so, maybe less. No swimming, no baths. Showers are okay. No tampons, no douches, nothing vaginally. And no intercourse before the discharge stops, either. Do you understand?"

How should you answer this? There is so much you don't understand, after all.

"Do you need a follow-up appointment with the doctor? You need to think about what form of birth control you'll be using. Afterwards." She looks at you pointedly.

You know you're supposed to respond. *Will you go back to the method that so clearly let you down* is what she's saying, isn't it? It's hard to figure out. The pills make you feel strange. You want to tell her you know how this whole thing works, you use a diaphragm. The only time you don't, the only time you allow yourself the freedom to be completely natural is when you are menstruating and the week afterwards. But this once, you got the dates wrong. Turns out that this one time, it had been twelve days since your period. A small mistake. A mistake that is currently forming gills and a neural tube, a mistake an inch long, maybe less. It seemed so minor at the time, one of those statistical things. Like the Space Shuttle. Worked perfectly, nineteen times out of twenty. But that twentieth launch, like the *Challenger*'s finale, what a doozie.

You have no idea how you've come to be lying on this meagre bed, no recollection of getting out of the orange moulded plastic chair and transiting to the operating room. The illumination here is bright as klieg lights. You try hard not to think about where they'll be blazing any second: where the sun don't shine. You spy the doctor. He is gowned, gloved, and masked, his trappings the white of a nuclear-flash. You didn't notice, during that preliminary assessment appointment, the hard glitter in his eyes. He holds his hands up, level with his shoulders, elbows bent. A crazy thought enters your head: he's like a priest. A "hello," croaks out of you. He doesn't say anything, not one single word. Maybe you didn't actually say anything either, you begin to think.

The film *Dead Ringers* flashes before your eyes. Too bad, you think. You used to like Jeremy Irons. Now maybe you've become him, the monster who invades the holy of holies with grotesque metal implements and murderous intentions.

A nurse materializes at your left side. "Hold my hand," she says, taking your hand in hers. "Squeeze it hard as you need to. Tell me if anything hurts too much." Her eyes are brown, as is her hair, her skin. Everything else is a sparkling white. They could make a commercial for laundry soap in here, you think, no problem.

You realize no one has smiled at you since you arrived.

Your feet are in the stirrups: back in the saddle again. A sucking sound becomes audible. The speculum pops you open, the doctor injects something into your cervix. How long is the needle, you wonder. How lucky you are to know anatomy, to understand what is happening, you think.

Or maybe not.

Your certainty wavers.

You know the procedure: the doctor introduces several small rods to your cervix in sequence, each one larger in diameter. You feel nothing beyond the cotton wool stuffing your brain.

The sucking sound is variegated now, like it's found something to hold on to, some meaning, what it's meant to take away. You work hard to avoid imagining a glass jar on the floor filling with multicolour tissue and fluids.

You hold the nurse's hand, give it one hard squeeze as a single monstrous contraction lurches through your lower abdomen, like productive labour minus the foreplay. You gasp, tears fill your eyes. You think this is good, *good*, it should hurt, why not?

And then, without a word, he steps away from you. The nurse watches closely, her latexed hand still touching yours.

"That's it," she says, "it's over. You can get up now."

Suddenly, you discover how cold you are. Your thighs are shaking, your legs have been uncomfortably jackknifed far too long. The nurse helps you up. The doctor has vanished.

The luminous sheet which you've just lain upon confronts you, a single glistening crimson globule marking the cloth. It takes your breath away. It is the most beautiful colour you've ever seen, and it's shaped like a teardrop.

You consider yanking the sheet from the gurney and taking it with you, whipping it round your shoulders like a witch's cape or a burial shroud.

And then, you see it as a different emblem of your changed life. You imagine it drenched in sunshine, hanging proudly outside your parents' home, the day after the wedding, centuries ago. Its lacy edges dance, gently ruffled by the breeze.

PATERNITY

"Sure you'll be alright?"

"Of course. She's a baby, not a nuclear reactor. It's a stretch, but I think I may just be able to handle her on my own."

Kate eyed him for a moment then said in a flat voice as she turned away, "Don't make fun of me for caring, okay?"

"I'm sorry," Jed offered, contrite. "I'll call your mother if I need anything." But he knew he wouldn't. Jed was looking forward to solo parenting for the three days Kate would be in New York, auditioning.

Kate scooped up flaxen-curled Daisy, kissed her cheek, her neck, the soft soft juncture where neck met shoulder. Daisy chortled, squirming as she was handed over to Jed.

"I'd better go; the taxi will be waiting," Kate said. She then delivered the final briefing, enumerating each point on the fingers of one hand: "Breast milk's in the freezer, formula's in the cupboard. Remember to mash a hard-boiled yolk in her cereal. And don't forget: we're trying zucchini this week."

"Yeah, yeah, will you just go already," he said, settling the baby on his hip.

Kate hefted the fuchsia suit bag to her shoulder, leaning over a bit for balance.

"Wait." Jed moved in and pulled her close, kissed her open-mouthed. "Don't forget about me," he said, breathing her in. He loved the smell of her, cloves and cardamom, never flowers.

"How could I," Kate murmured. There was laughter in her voice, but already she had moved beyond his embrace and when the door closed behind her, it carried a surprising finality.

Jed brought Daisy to the windows that wrapped two sides of the large rectangular apartment, trying to see the street down below, trying to find the taxi with Kate in it. But the effort was futile; the apartment was up too high. He jiggled the baby, kissing the top of her head, calling her his butterball as they moved back to the dining area.

"Here we go, then," he said, settling the butterball back into her highchair and launched into the running monologue of the parent-of-an-infant: part stream of consciousness, part language stimulation. "Well, that's it, Daisy. Mommy's off to the airport. It's just the two of us now. First, we'll clean up the breakfast dishes, then we'll get dressed and go out. What would you like to do today?" He paused, leaving room for her to participate in the conversation, just in case Daisy, precocious at nine months, was suddenly capable of answering.

Oblivious, she gurgled on, pushing cereal circles around her tray. Her spoon clattered to the floor. Daisy peered over at the noise, then looked up at him, brown eyes wide, her eyebrows question marks.

"Okay, then," Jed said, "I'll decide."

Jed had booked three days off work because Kate's agent, pushing her to get back in the game, had arranged a series of readings in New York.

"A couple of plays, an animated film, even an audition for spokesbabe of a cosmetic line aimed at new mothers: fading stretch marks, firming sagging breasts, that sort of thing. I just hope they've got something for the bags under my eyes," Kate told him when she initially broached the subject of New York. She had looked at him, on the defensive, unsure of his reaction. How long was he planning on holding a grudge against an entire city, she'd asked. Couldn't he see that this was important for her career?

Of course, he agreed. Though it marked the first time they would be separated since the baby. In fact, over the course of their four-year relationship, they had only been apart once, during that six-week interlude two years ago. Jed pushed the thought away. He took the espresso maker from the stove, twisted it apart, and dumped the grounds in the bin beneath the sink.

That evening, Daisy was on her tummy on the living room floor, surrounded by toys. She swam around, backwards mostly, not quite crawling. Ella crooned, "How lonnnng has this been goin' onnn?" Jed poured himself a glass of bordeaux, *appellation d'origine controlée*. He settled into the luxurious upholstery. Lamplight created reflecting pools on the polished hardwood.

Jed was the manager of a successful venture fund. From a slim leather briefcase he pulled out a prospectus and started paging through it.

> Today's first-time parents are the oldest in North American history. And where previous generations were birthed by women in their early twenties, new mothers these days are often a decade older. This is a true social revolution, related partly to the increase in women's pursuit of higher education and careers. Since we know fertility declines with age, it's no wonder the number of couples requiring assistance to achieve conception has skyrocketed. For fifteen years, we at Creation Incorporated have helped families happen…

Yada, yada, yada, Jed thought, but he granted that these people might actually be on to something. Many couples he and Kate knew had consulted fertility specialists. And he figured there were others among their circle keeping it quiet, suffering through a misplaced sense of shame.

When they first came calling, Creation Incorporated's power-suited principals had explained that starting out, they'd discovered a niche in paternity testing. They called it their "DNA for the divorce market." Jed found that a cold-hearted expression, but he'd dealt with scientists before, knew they didn't always have the greatest people skills. They had come to him looking for capital, bullish on "the fertility-enhancement side" of the business. Jed always considered optimism a good sign. Still, he couldn't shake the feeling that it was all a little unsavoury somehow, this commodification of family. Jed was a pretty matter-of-fact guy, but even he thought some things might be sacred.

> Domestic adoption can't keep pace with demand, and foreign adoptions can be difficult, with costs easily ballooning beyond $30,000. A recent survey found that an overwhelming majority of would-be parents prefer the idea of medical assistance to have their own children, and they are *very* motivated. Creation Incorporated is dedicated to providing these consumers what they truly seek: cost-effective, natural parenting.

Enough of *this* shit, Jed thought. His gaze wandered to the baby and he smiled. Lately, he'd felt the old conundrums resurfacing, bubbling up like gases from a deepwater vent. Kate was hardly sympathetic. "Mind farts," she told him. She'd roll her eyes and suggest he "take up sailing or run a marathon, or something." There were times – years at a stretch – when Jed lived in the moment, enjoying every second of his alpha male existence. Those were the periods he imagined himself free of all those clichés regarding "meaning." But somehow, the questions always found their way back, like lost pets in a Disney movie. Daisy was his best refuge yet. Just looking at her calmed him, holding her – feeling her wriggle, warm and alive – reassured him to his very chromosomes: there were some realities larger than his own small life.

Jed looked up as Daisy started to cry, wedged immobile between the armchair and an end table. "I'm coming sweetie," he cooed. He picked her up and kissed her, smoothed her tears away.

In the middle of the night, Jed awoke, heart pounding. It was that dream again, the one that had stalked him since Daisy was born. She was wailing, alone and afraid, and he hacked through jungle-dense foliage, knowing all the while that his search was hopeless. That in the darkness, she was lost to him. Each time he had the dream, he'd waken wretched with the need to find her, tears tightening his throat.

The baby monitor glowed in the dark like a dragon's eye. Jed listened closely. He didn't hear a sound.

Kate had called that night, from a cast party. "Opening night," she'd told him. In the background Jed heard music and throaty laughter. When he told her it sounded like the usual drunken debauchery, Kate got short with him and terminated the conversation.

They never spoke of the affair. Kate grew furious if he even mentioned it. It was over, she had decreed, all ancient history. So, closing on two years later, the breach between them has sealed. Jed worked to smooth it over, doing his best to pretend it never happened. But in dark moments, he gauged that the probability Daisy was actually "of his flesh" at fifty percent.

He had never before considered testing Daisy's paternity, but now the thought slithered cold through his consciousness, doubt and misgiving a coiled double helix inside him. He adored the baby and he loved Kate, in his sadly hopeful way. He'd forgiven her – as much as he was able to – anyway. But he hadn't forgotten, at least not yet. And every so often, when there was too much time to think, the affair sandbagged him.

Would it matter if Daisy wasn't his biological daughter? Jed didn't know, but he was also afraid to find out. He had the sense, sometimes, that he was walking a tightrope over a precipice, flirting with disaster. Just a few wrong words, he thought, and it could be the end of everything.

Next morning, while Daisy banged a wooden spoon on the floor, Jed sat fingering his Blackberry. He recalled a number from the cell phone's coltan and silicon bowels and engaged it, cursing himself silently. It rang several times. Before he could say anything, he was on hold, enduring something by The Tragically Hip. He sighed then and hung up. A flash of anger moved through him, there and gone, like heat lightening. *What was this adolescent shit?* Jed took a few cleansing breaths, Kate's prescription for stress, gleaned from Lamaze class and her years of yoga. But he was far from pacific, and his mind's eye conjured the image of Kate, gripping the brass bedstead, head thrown back, her lithe golden body naked and erotically arched. Being ministered to by someone else.

He dialled again and this time was almost immediately connected directly to his contact at the company. "I would like to know," Jed said, head bowed, thumb and forefinger pinching the bridge of his nose, "how a paternity test is performed."

Dieter sounded surprised, then determined not to be. "Well, we draw some blood from the child and the parent in question. We only need a little, five millilitres. The DNA is amplified directly from that and then sequenced. After that, we compare the patterns. The whole thing can be done in twenty-four, maybe thirty-six hours."

"Couldn't you use a cheek swab? Some hair or something?"

"No. Most people think this is the case, but they have been watching too many crime shows. If you want to be certain – and let me tell you, our clients do – you need more material than that."

Jed rang off distractedly, the word "blood" ringing in his ears.

That night, he called Kate's cell every hour on the hour between 9:00 p.m. and 2:00 a.m., but she never answered.

The next morning, Daisy woke fussy, and Jed felt just as out of sorts. Could be she's teething, he thought. Well, if he had to cancel brunch at Charlie and Daniella's, he would. If it was better for her, he didn't mind hanging around the apartment. He thought it might help if he kept her close for a while. He put on a CD Kate had bought recently – *Mozart for Babies: Sleepy Time* – and spent much of the morning in the rocking chair, reading to her or just holding Daisy quietly, her head against his shoulder, her chubby little hand crammed into her rosebud mouth. He patted her velour-covered bottom, he massaged her back. From time to time as they swayed, Jed rubbed his cheek absently against the side of her head and sniffed her hair. She smelled like almonds.

Later, out on the street, the warmth of the sun like a benediction, Daisy babbled and crowed, smacking her hands on his shoulders and kicking her legs. Jed took these as caresses. His phone went off and he recognized Kate's ring.

"Hello, baby. How are you? I miss you." The warmth in her voice travelled right down his spine. "I'm not used to sleeping alone."

"I tried to get you a few times last night."

"I know, I'm sorry. I left my phone in the back of a cab."

"And you got it back?"

"You better believe it, baby. New York has changed."

"I guess it must have."

"How's my little girl? Missing her mommy?" Kate sounded pouty, the way she did sometimes when they made love. Jed felt a pull in his groin.

"She told me to tell you she's scarred for life," he said.

"Jed!"

"She's fine, Kate. Peeing, pooping. A regular prodigy."

"You wouldn't believe how much I miss her. I'm expressing milk like crazy, and still, my boobs are swollen and sore."

"Wish I was there to make them feel better."

"Uh-huh."

"How's it going, work wise?"

"Oh, you know, Paul's noncommittal, says we're just here to do the rounds, show the flag."

"Really? Things sounded more definite than that before you left."

"Don't be bringing me down, Jed. I have to be up, up, up for this, you know I do."

"Well, you sound good. A little manic maybe, but good."

"Manic? That I can live with. Let me speak to my baby girl, won't you?"

"Okay." Jed removed the backpack and held the phone so that Daisy could hear her.

"You have to try this, Jed," Charlie called from the kitchen. "Iranian dates stuffed with warm Cambozola."

"Sounds good, but I can't eat another bite." Jed heard the opening and closing of cupboards. From his spot on the sofa, he kept an eye on two-year-old Harry who was seated near Daisy, on a sheepskin rug. They weren't playing together but he could tell that they were aware of each other. It seemed to Jed that every primary-coloured plastic baby toy in existence was scattered around the living room.

Daniella walked in with the French press and refilled his mug.

"Thank you, that's great," he said, inhaling deeply.

"It always tastes better when someone else does the cooking," Daniella said. She noticed Jed watching the children and said, "Don't worry, Harry's gentle with the little ones." She patted the curve of her belly. "Well, he better be. This one will be here before you know it." The microwave pinged. "How's Kate? You getting along okay without her?"

"Daisy's fine, but I seem to have taken up talking to myself."

"You're supposed to talk to them. All the time. That's how their language develops."

"Even when she's sleeping?"

"Now you're just ragging me."

Charlie breezed in with the plate of dates and cheese. He stopped to kiss Daniella's cheek. "'A ship under sail and a big-bellied woman are the handsomest two things that can be seen common,'" he announced. "Benjamin Franklin."

"Next, you'll be wanting a sailboat, I suppose," Daniella said. "That's his favourite quotation these days. Honestly, he never shuts up."

"Tell me about it," Jed said.

"A sailboat – what a fine idea, my darling. It's just the right time to take up an expensive new hobby, what with all that leisure time I'll have once the baby arrives."

"Sit down, you," she said, shooing him away. She deposited the carafe on the coffee table and returned to the kitchen.

"She is so great," Jed said.

"Don't I know it." Charlie settled his bulk into a chair that was crooked at a ninety-degree angle to Jed. "And, more important, she knows that I know. Try one of these." He reached over and popped a date into his mouth. "So," he mumbled, "how's it going?"

"Great, just great."

"I was wondering..."

"What?"

Charlie said nothing.

"It's a business trip," said Jed.

"Uh-huh."

"Besides, it's good to have this time with Daisy, one-on-one."

Charlie cocked his head to one side and said, "O-kaaay."

Jed leaned forward to get to the dates. "Mm," he said, "you're right, these are good."

"You're changing the subject."

"You're nuts, you know that?"

"I've seen that look before."

"That's not a look. That's my face."

"Okay, forget it. I shouldn't have mentioned it," Charlie said.

You got that right, Jed thought. As soon as he could, he excused himself. In the bathroom, he took a good long look in the mirror.

That night, he tried Kate again. He called at 9:00 p.m, 10:00 p.m., and at 12:30 a.m. before he gave up, tossing and turning for the better part of an hour before dropping off to sleep.

In the morning, Kate called from a restaurant. "How're you doing?"

"We're good. Lose your phone again?" There were loud voices and clanking dishes.

"Very funny, baby. I don't always hear it in those crowd scenes."

"What if there'd been an emergency?"

"Come on, Jed. Daisy's okay, isn't she?"

"She's fine, Kate. She may be teething again. She's drooling like mad, and she was a little grumpy yesterday."

"The poor sweetie! Did she keep you from sleeping last night?"

No, Jed wanted to say, if anyone kept me up last night it was you. "No, she slept like a baby. And how are you?"

"I'm wiped, actually. I've kind of forgotten what it's like – up all night, sleeping half the day."

"All night?"

"Paul insisted on doing three events last night, it was ridiculous. He introduced me to a guy who's doing a reading of a new Tracy Letts play."

"Who?"

"Tracy Letts. Pulitzer Prize, Tony Award? An opportunity like that… it could mean years of work."

"Sounds great."

Jed realized he was pacing. He plopped down on the sofa. What kind of a life could they have if she was down there for years, working all night and sleeping all day? And why on earth hadn't they discussed this before she left, before she even made plans to fly down there? Because they never discussed anything beyond the short-term. Because he knew she was dreaming those old New York dreams and he was afraid of what might happen if he woke her up. Tell me that you miss me, he thought, swallowing hard. "Who else was there?"

And Kate was off, naming names, describing hairstyles, enumerating fashion faux pas. Who was sleeping with who, who was hot and who was not.

After he got off the phone, he paced again. He ran his hands through his hair, then shoved them in his pockets. What, exactly, was going on here, and what was he prepared to do about it? Was he going to just let things go on like this, with Kate calling all the shots? What if she got one of those parts Paul was trying to massage her into? Would she take Daisy away with her? When the hell had he gotten so passive? He looked at his watch. Daisy had been napping two hours already. Maybe he should check on her, make sure she was still breathing. It wasn't the sort of thought that usually occurred to him. He went into the darkened room and found Daisy curled on her side, her back to him. He hesitated, put a hand out and touched her, was moved by her quick little breaths.

Back in the living room, he tripped over the briefcase, eased halfway beneath the chesterfield. DNA for the divorce market. Knowledge is power. Who said that? Right, Francis Bacon. The bastard. How could Jed fight for Daisy if she wasn't his? He picked up his briefcase and sent it crashing into a floor lamp. Too bad, he'd clean it up later. He checked the time and again rang the VP Finance at Creation Incorporated. Jed spoke quietly, walking over to the window, drumming his fingers on the sill. He fixed a time the next morning for him and Daisy to go in and have their blood drawn, then he holstered his phone. It was just an appointment, he told himself. He didn't have to go through with it.

His cell phone rang as he was getting the baby ready for the trip downtown. He let Kate go to voicemail, and wrestled Daisy into some warm clothes. "C'mon, my dear," he said, picking her up, kissing her, and buckling her into the backpack.

On the bus, people smiled at them as Daisy burbled through the fifteen-minute ride. When she complained in the elevator of the downtown tower, he bounced a little to humour her. Once on the 16th floor, Jed quickly ducked through the doorway, casting a brief glance over his shoulder as he entered Creation Incorporated. A receptionist paged Dieter who materialized in his $3,000 suit to shake Jed's hand, make appreciative noises about Daisy, and walk them to the treatment room.

A white-coated technician arrived and Dieter left them to it, saying, "This should only take a few minutes. Ask Ella at reception to bring you to my office when you're done. We can talk then." He shook Jed's hand again and was gone.

The technician labelled some tubes. "I'd like you to take my blood first," Jed said, placing Daisy, still in the backpack, on a chair. His palms were sweaty.

"No problem," the other man said.

Jed removed his jacket and rolled up his sleeve.

Daisy's head swivelled, her eyes wide open, taking the place in.

"Hey, baby, baby," Jed sang, and Daisy rewarded him with a big smile.

The tech said, "Take a seat here, please." He gestured to the examination table, then tied some tubing around Jed's arm. "It's just like any other blood test. Clench and unclench your hand a few times, so the vein pops up. That's it. You've got great veins."

"How do you get the baby to do that?"

"Hang on now, let's get this done first, and then we can talk."

Jed nodded and took a breath. The cold alcohol wipe startled him. The gloved finger probing his distended blood vessel. And the glinting needle – he usually looked away – followed by the surprising pain of the puncture. Thick dark liquid gushed into the purple-stoppered tube. After a moment, the technician pulled the needle back and taped some gauze to Jed's inner elbow, telling him to apply pressure for a minute, to prevent bruising.

"All right now, can we get the baby out of there? Take her clothes off too, that's usually the easiest."

"Sure thing," Jed said. His heart was beating double-time. He unbuckled the backpack's halter, pulled Daisy out and kissed her, then laid her on the examination table and stripped her to her pink cotton onesie. Daisy put a hand to her mouth. She didn't look happy. "Okay," Jed said. When he looked up, the tech was holding a plastic restraint device with Velcro straps.

"Let me pop just her in here, we'll be done in a minute."

"You have to strap her down?"

"It's really the safest way."

"Are you..." Jed's voice trailed off.

"Why don't you sit in reception for a sec? I'll call you right back when we're done." He smiled and picked up the baby.

Jed went into the hallway.

The technician turned and placed Daisy on the plastic board, fastened the attachments. Daisy squirmed and squawked, her face reddening. The technician pushed the door shut with his foot.

Jed stood there, listening to Daisy protest. He jiggled the doorknob but it was locked. "Hey," he said. Then he said it again, louder this time. A head poked out of a nearby office. Jed banged on the door. "Let's just forget about this, okay?" he shouted, pulling on the doorknob again.

The door swung inward to expose Daisy, red and screaming, and the flushed technician.

"Forget it," Jed said, walking in and pushing the young man aside. "I've changed my mind, okay? Tell Dieter I'll call him."

The other man awkwardly backed out of the small room.

"Shh, sweetheart," Jed crooned. He took Daisy in his arms, cradling her against him. He wanted to sing "You Are My Sunshine," but it proved incompatible with the desire to punch the technician's lights out. All Jed could manage was a feeble croaking. Still, it seemed to do the trick.

Twenty minutes later, man and child descended from the bus, a few stops early. Jed hoped a walk would do him good; he still felt ready to pull someone's head off. A few stray drops made him glance up at the clouds. Daisy, exhausted by her ordeal, dozed in the backpack. Her head lolled forward, her curls brushing Jed's neck. He crossed at Cote des Neiges and Queen Mary Road. Falling leaves sketched lazy arcs, collecting in amber curb-side puddles. Jed took another deep breath, willing himself to relax.

The huge green dome of St. Joseph's Oratory, Montreal's best-known shrine, loomed on the hillside before him. He had never been inside it, despite having lived nearby the better part of a decade. Today was as good a time as any, he figured. Maybe he could also avoid the rain.

Before the Oratory, three staircases in front beckoned up up up, the middle one sporting wooden planks over its cement treads. A discreet sign designated it for the penitent. He watched as several pilgrims mounted on their knees, clutching rosaries, reciting a prayer at each step. Jed didn't want to know what motivated someone to climb the stairs that way. He was certain it could only be a catastrophe. And this, he didn't want to think about. He felt close enough to the contours of disaster already.

Jed took the stairs two at a time, passing everyone. Life in the fast lane, he thought. Beyond the heavy oak doors was an escalator that delivered him up and into the cavernous Oratory. There, people milled about in small clusters and spoke in whispers, keeping their children close by. The air felt cold and clammy. A ring of windows at the height of the dome provided illumination, the interior a curious combination of the permanent and the provisional – walls of grey stone, seating comprised of folding chairs; the fixtures whispered Art Deco while a huge backlit cross surveyed the scene, flanked by immense banners of blood-red cloth. Jed wandered past the Stations of the Cross and then left with a sense of relief.

Coming out the oak doors, Jed noticed a stream of people snaking through a small doorway labelled The Crypt Church, and allowed himself to be swept along, into the twilight of a long low room with a rounded ceiling, like a cylinder tipped on one side. People dipped their fingers in the white marble font, drawing the sign of the cross across their chests. On his left, an archway revealed a room of guttering candles. To his right, dark pews led to a wooden altar decorated with gold leaf. He moved that way. People were everywhere, some sitting in pews, others kneeling – individuals, couples, families, every age and culture.

Jed removed the baby pack and settled down beside it, flexing his shoulders with some pleasure, enjoying the sensation of a burden lifted. Daisy still slept. Jed felt something ticking inside him. He couldn't say if it was guilt or love, anger or fear. It was all that and none of that, alpha and omega, everything mixed together. The immensity of the Oratory, he suddenly understood, was just for show, like a grand parlour nobody ever entered. This place was more human in dimension, more like the kitchen, the heart of a home.

Beside the altar, under a spotlight, his gaze fell on a painted statue, larger-than-life. It appeared to have been carved from a single tree trunk, a man in robes holding close a young child. Both had crowns, both had haloes.

It took Jed a moment to grasp that this was St. Joseph, foster father, holding Someone Else's son – but when he did, his heart leapt. Devotion pierced him.

Daisy wailed, waking abruptly, a woman in the pew in front turned at the sound. Her hair was pulled into a long braid, black and shiny. "Is that your daughter?" she asked. A small jewel glittered in one nostril and her accent spoke of India.

"Yes," he answered, focused on freeing Daisy from her constraints.

"What a lovely child," the woman told him.

Daisy cried in earnest as Jed, flustered, worked on unbuckling her and taking her in his arms. He wanted to answer the woman – to thank her – but by the time he turned back, the woman had already moved out of his universe and returned to her own.

In the darkness, Jed held Daisy close as she fussed, rubbing her back, pressing his lips against the softness of her temple. He breathed in the baby-smell of her, that sweet milky yeastiness, like something growing and expanding, filling all the emptiness in the world. He inhaled until he had to let out a long sigh.

"There, now," he murmured. Soothing her, he couldn't help but notice that her tears tasted exactly like his own.

LIGHTER THAN AIR

Sandra caught the light at the intersection of Monkland and Decarie, only to have the minivan plunge into gridlock as she rounded the corner. "Shit," she exclaimed. "Well, congratulations, Dan. You've managed to elevate procrastination to an art form. Fifteen minutes last week. We're definitely beating that today."

"I hate going there," Dan groused. "He's always saying, 'Tell me how you feel.' I've told him, 'Every time I come here, it's one more hour shaved off my life.'"

It was April, which marked two solid months of Dan's resistance.

"You're twenty-two," Sandra said. "You keep vampire hours, refuse to go to school or look for a job. You're either depressed or an asshole and for $120 an hour, this guy's going to figure out which." Sandra was aware that talking to her son this way disqualified her from any Mother of the Year awards. The things she said to him – she regretted them as soon as they poured from her mouth, but she just couldn't seem to help herself. "Honest to God, Dan, some day we'll both need therapy, just for these trips to the shrink's."

He had been a crier. She had nursed him for hours, twining her fingers through his auburn curls. She'd adored him, felt as though the milk was her love made manifest. She would have done anything for him. And now… she lifted her eyes from the road and took in the grotty t-shirt beneath the navy hoodie, the grey stubble and lavender smudges beneath his bleary eyes. She reached a hand towards the lank brown hair hanging over his face, but Dan recoiled before she could touch him.

She wrinkled her nose. "When was the last time you washed your hair or took a shower?"

"Love you, too, Ma," Dan said. A white ear bud lay on his shoulder, the other anchoring him to his MP3 player. Sandra heard the annoying crash of cymbals. These kids, living lives accompanied by their own personal soundtracks.

"You waste your life on that sofa, channel surfing." She blasted the horn as a red sports car cut in front of her. "Selfish bastard," she growled. "I just don't want you ending up like your cousin."

"Who?" he said.

"Cheryl. She was hospitalized twice last year, doesn't even remember the first time. Imagine. She's been getting electroshock therapy every month for a couple of years now. Must be lots she doesn't remember."

"What for?"

"Eh?" Sandra pressed again on the horn.

"The shock therapy. What's it for?"

"Oh, you know. 'Bad thoughts,' she calls them. About killing herself."

"You don't believe her?"

"I think she's just trying to punish her parents for something they don't even know they've done."

"I can't imagine anything shock therapy could make better," Dan said.

The red light had pinned them beside a new big box mall. Sandra craned her neck to look up at the series of inflatables that decked the exterior of the building. Bearing the bright colours and patterns of hot air balloons, they screamed: *Soldes!* and *Rabais!* as they swayed overhead, straining against invisible tethers. The light went green. As she eased back into the traffic, Sandra found herself struggling to focus. She felt something like panic – her heart thumping madly, her throat constricting, a sweaty sheen blooming on her face. "Well, if holding a knife to your wrist for a couple of seconds means you need to be hospitalized, you can bet most of us do," Sandra said. "I could use a little time off myself."

"Does it really matter what you think?"

Sandra banged on the steering wheel and turned to glare at her son. "They say these things run in families, did you know that, Dan? See any parallels here?" Really, part of her wondered, how far would she go? Damn, damn, damn. She hated herself for this verbal diarrhea.

"Maybe. I just haven't tried to kill myself yet," he said.

"Well, thank God for small miracles. Just quit fucking with your life like this."

"Ever occur to you that it's my life? If I fuck it up, that's my choice. My choice, Ma. Nothing to do with you. Nothing at all."

"If you ever have a child, you'll know why I can never accept that." She imagined Dan and the psychologist together, gazing out the window in companionable silence at those bobbling balloons. She jolted to the curb in front of an unadorned beige office building. The pounding in her chest abated, Sandra felt relieved that Dan would be someone else's problem for an hour. "Maybe next week you'll take the bus, okay? I can't take this anymore. The traffic kills me," she said.

Dan had the door open before the van was completely stopped. Jumping out, he spat, "See ya, Ma," before sending the door crashing into its frame. The minivan jumped back into traffic, tires squealing. Sandra shook her head. She couldn't blame Dan for slamming the door, not a bit.

"Middle age," Sandra said to Jillian. "I look back and see, if not failure exactly, just a notable lack of success." They were on the *terrasse* of a crowded bistro, everyone hungry for the sun as Montreal emerged sharply into spring. Sandra dug through her purse for sunglasses, came up empty-handed and sighed.

Jillian reached for the bottle sweating on the table and poured more wine in their glasses. "Don't be thinking so hard all the time," Jillian said. "One day you're going to hurt yourself."

"Hunh. Your life's so uncomplicated. Divorced, no kids. You do what you want, when you want."

"Right. And if I died tomorrow, it might be a week before anyone noticed. And after they did, most of them'd hardly pay me more than an occasional thought. But do I really give a shit? This is who I am, take it or shove it." Jillian pulled a crushed box of cherry-flavoured cigarillos from her bag. A man in his twenties at the next table offered her a light with a Gallic flourish.

Jillian continued, "A son who's failed to launch, a husband spending all his time on the other side of the world, a research job going down the drain. Cry me a river. As stories go, yours is hardly a tragedy. You've got all your limbs, most of your brain cells. Isn't there anything you've ever dreamt of doing? This is it, dammit. We're not going to get many more chances."

Sandra slid a cherry tomato around in the dregs of its balsamic dressing. "All I ever wanted to do was research, have my own lab. I thought I'd be saving the world, you know?" After she'd obtained her Master's degree, Sandra had been thrilled to find work creating a mouse model of diabetes. She'd thought it was important work. She'd been so sure then it would lead to a cure, that all her efforts would be building something worthwhile. But from her current vantage point, it all now seemed so inconsequential. All she had done was prove the disease settled in layers, which she would then excavate, like an archaeologist. "And to think I killed thousands of mice just for that..." Sometimes Sandra thought of her career as a murine holocaust, herself a pied piper followed by hordes of pirouetting headless white mice.

The waiter placed steaming plates of pasta before them. Sandra watched Jillian and the waiter make the grinding of pepper and the grating of parmesan sexually suggestive. Jillian's cigarillo lay in an ashtray, its sweet smoke rising in a lazy spiral.

When the waiter left, Sandra said, "How do you do that?"

"Do what?"

"Forget it." She sighed. She sipped her wine, twirled noodles round her fork, then put down the utensil. "I just never thought things would turn out this way. I had so many plans."

"You got pregnant and gave up on having your own lab."

"You make it sound like I did it on purpose."

"You said it, I didn't."

"Shit happens. I made the responsible choice, didn't I? Isn't that what being an adult's all about?"

"Honey, we're each of us a work in progress. Stop being so hard on yourself." Jillian caught the eye of the man with the lighter and smiled.

Sandra made a little moue and took a pull from her wineglass. "There's this new guy at the institute, works in psychogenetics."

Jillian raised an eyebrow.

"He gave a lecture on the genetic predisposition to suicide. Hemingway's the classic example: his father killed himself and so did two of Hemingway's siblings, one of his kids, even his granddaughter, Margaux. Anyhow, this guy asked me to work with him."

"It's an important subject."

"It means starting over."

"But you've got the technical smarts he needs, right?"

"Yeah," Sandra conceded. "He's got a collection of brain tissue samples from suicide victims. He wants to do expression studies, says I could even do a PhD with him if I want."

"Sounds perfect. He needs you, you need a job."

Sandra busied herself with her fettuccine for a moment. "It's just… starting over like this makes me feel I've wasted the last twenty years."

"Oh, for God's sake, Sandra. You said it: shit happens. Sometimes you just have to roll with it."

Sandra sighed again and tapped her fingernails on the marble tabletop. "All right, enough about me. Tell me what you've been up to, lately."

"Did I tell you I met this guy online a few weeks ago?"

"No. And? Have you slept with him yet?"

Jillian laughed and stabbed the half-smoked cigarillo into the remains of her pasta. "Not quite, but I'm thinkin' he's definitely sponge-worthy."

By mid-May, Sandra was trying to absorb some fifty scientific articles about suicide: genetic and protein variants of tryptophan hydroxylase, serotonin transport proteins, the psychology of suicidal ideation, and theories on impulsiveness, loss and resilience. Many nights she sat alone in her living room with a glass of Pinot Grigio, ploughing through reviews clogged with pedigrees, surprised to discover that suicide rivalled breast cancer as a cause of death, that nearly ten times as many Canadians killed themselves as died from murder or AIDS. It astounded her to discover an epidemic of such scope and yet, such discretion. Sandra learned the jargon, the difference between "attempters," "completers," and "survivors," the latter being the mourners left behind by a "successful" suicide.

In late May, Liam returned home for a couple of weeks and kept harping on all the details he'd left hanging in Tianjin. He was gambling everything on this venture – their savings and home equity, money borrowed from her parents – all to set up a plastics factory that would make desks modelled after the hoods of Formula One race cars.

It was past midnight. The two of them moved between the bathroom and the bedroom. Water ran in short bursts. The house held its breath.

"The guy from Wal-Mart loved our presentation. If they bite, we could make a real killing," Liam said.

"Mm-hmm," said Sandra. She'd heard all this before.

"Come with me this time, Sandra," he said, just as he had before every other trip he'd taken in the past eighteen months. And Sandra responded the way she always did. Their conversations played out as though scripted, the sighs, pauses and harsh words appearing right on cue.

"We've been through this. I can't. I'm wrapping things up in the old lab, trying to get up to speed with the new stuff. And Dan's so messed up right now."

"He's not a kid anymore, Sandra. He's twenty-one—"

"Twenty-two," she corrected him.

"He's old enough to stay on his own. Maybe it would do him good to have you out of his business for a while, ever think of that?"

"Dan needs me," she said.

"What if I need you? Your lab's closing anyway. Wouldn't this be the perfect time to take a break?"

For a moment, there was silence. "You can be a real bastard sometimes," she finally said. "It's trivial to you, my lab shutting down. But for me it's the end of something huge."

"Come with me this time, Sandy. Please. It'd be good for us." Maybe if he'd said this while holding her, Sandra might have recognized his plea for what it was. Instead, Liam slipped his polo shirt over his head, unzipping and stepping out of his khakis and boxers. He was still attractive: his middle had thickened but his pecs were well defined, he still had most of his hair, and she'd always relished the strength in his thighs. He slid into bed and propped himself up on the pillows.

"Good for you, you mean," Sandra said, putting his shirt and underwear in the white wicker basket, shaking his pants into their creases and hanging them in the closet. "You'll be busy with the thousand and one things only you can handle. And there I'll be, completely isolated, unable even to speak to anyone, in a place that couldn't possibly be more foreign."

"If anyone imagines there's a thousand and one things only they can take care of, it's you, babe." Liam, his reading half-glasses perched on his nose, peered over the top of *The Economist* at her. "Is it so terrible to want you in my bed every night?"

Another of Sandra's sore points: Liam arrived home after weeks away expecting a Stepford wife, expecting a virtual fuck-a-thon. "You want me in bed, you know where I am, dammit," she said. What about all those nights he was away when she wanted sex? "You're the one chasing some goddam fantasy. And even when you are here, you're not really with us. You're really still back there, dreaming." Sandra had put on an old pair of flannel pyjamas and a white tank top. She scooped some aloe cream from the jar on the night table and rubbed it hard into her skin. A green scent filled the air.

"I'm just trying to build something. For all of us."

"Thanks but no thanks, okay? My life is here. I can't just blow it off because you nurture some pathetic pipe dream."

The silence was so sudden, it made her ears ring. Sandra noisily closed the white jar, returned it to the night table. She turned out the light and got into bed. Oh shit, oh shit, she thought.

Liam's glasses clattered as they hit the bedside table. His voice floated to her through the darkness: "If that's the way you feel, I won't mention it again."

It wasn't, not exactly. But all Sandra could say was, "So I hope that's settled, then."

They turned away from one another. The bedding rustled.

For the rest of his two weeks in Montreal, Liam and Sandra were overly polite, when they did speak to each other. Even Dan noticed. And though Sandra drove Liam to the airport, in itself an unusual event, she saw the hurt had settled in the soft brown depths of his eyes. When he left her to enter the security checkpoint, Sandra felt the prickling of tears. Why can't I just say I'm sorry, she asked herself. Why can't I just call him back?

The month that Liam was away, their emails and occasional phone calls had a perfunctory quality that left Sandra rattled. He was due back the last week in June, for their anniversary. Sandra decided to book a table at an Italian restaurant in Old Montreal they'd gone to on special occasions, ever since she proposed to him there.

She had herself waxed in anticipation. The esthetician had been pushing "the Brazilian" for months, and Sandra finally gave in, thinking maybe this would be a good thing, a little variety. As the wax was ripped from her body Sandra cursed, almost crying and yet somehow happy for the pain. She hated herself for having made them both so unhappy.

She offered an awkward apology when she met Liam at the airport: "I've been so short-tempered," she said, "what with the lab situation, Dan's shtick, you gone so much."

"Forget it," he told her, "I know it's been hard." But in bed they didn't touch each other, as though sex was some language they no longer shared.

Their anniversary fell on a Thursday, June 29th, a few days after the *Fête Nationale*. The night was perfect, warm, too early in the season to be humid, with a cool breeze coming up from the river. Throngs of people, Montreal natives and tourists alike, took *calèche* rides or strolled the narrow cobblestone streets, stopping to watch the fire eaters in the Place Jacques Cartier or goggle at the gold-lamé Elvis who stood like a statue, as the mimes handed balloons to the children and the musicians alternated the love songs of Daniel Bélanger with those of The Beatles. On the *ruelle des artistes*, the real thing occasionally shone among the charlatans who painted posters with watercolours and sold them for seventy-five dollars a pop.

When Liam and Sandra entered the restaurant, it was already filled with smiling couples and perfumed with garlic, rosemary, and candle wax. They were seated at a table covered with white linen and silver plate. Sandra was content, thinking she had stage-managed this well. Liam ordered their favourite wine for special occasions, a robust Le Serre Nuove dell'Ornellaia.

An hour later, he poured the last of it in their glasses. Conversation had been agreeably low-key: Liam's progress in China, Jillian's new boyfriend, Sandra's pleasure in discovering that Dan had taken up jogging. They discussed the possibility of her pursuing a PhD and whose parents they were due to visit at Christmas. She took another sip of wine, rolling it in her mouth, savouring its earthy bursts of chocolate and spice.

Liam put his glass down and lowered his eyes. "I have to tell you, Sandy… it wouldn't be fair not to. I've met someone, over there." He looked up at her as she choked on the wine and coughed. He handed his napkin to her then went on in a rush, "Dan's older now. We are too. Maybe we've changed, you know? Maybe we're just not on the same page anymore. These things happen."

Sandra was still spluttering; she dabbed at her mouth with her napkin, unable to speak. She coughed till there were tears in her eyes.

"We can be adult about this, though, can't we?" Liam went on. "Let's just take it from here and deal with whatever comes."

Sandra could only nod and look away. She felt for a moment as though she was hovering above her chair, as though she was about to float right up to the ceiling, as though gravity had ceased to be a force of nature. She brought the napkin up to the corner of each eye.

A young couple sat at the next table, leaning toward each other, the candlelight revealing a vital expectancy in their faces. They could have been Liam and herself, a lifetime ago. She felt suddenly there was something she must tell them, something urgent, but she wasn't quite sure what it was. But from that moment on, and for the rest of Liam's visit, Sandra had the obscure impression she was auditioning for the lead role in her own life.

In mid-July, Dan offered to make his own way to the psychologist's. Sandra took this as evidence he had finally engaged with the therapist and regained a sense of responsibility. It wasn't until she came home a couple of weeks later and took her messages from the answering machine that she realized something else might be going on. Dr. Lala's secretary had called to ask if Dan intended to keep his regular weekly booking. He had missed three consecutive appointments. "Please let us know as soon as possible, as Dr. Lala has a number of patients on a waiting list who would be pleased to take the appointment." Mulling it over, Sandra realized Dan had been out of the house a lot lately, too.

She confronted him the next time their paths crossed. He was in the kitchen, making himself a strawberry banana smoothie.

"Dr. Lala's office called earlier today," she said, looking him over. He was clean-shaven for a change, his hair and clothes neat and cared for, if you could forgive the oversize jeans threatening to drop to the floor any moment. He'd lost some weight. The jogging had firmed him up; his features were a little better defined, a little less like the Pillsbury doughboy's.

"I've been meaning to give you your cheques back," Dan said, intent on pouring the drink from the blender.

From a voluminous pocket he pulled out three envelopes – the cheques she'd given him for the psychologist. She took them and slowly unfolded them, then looked up at her son.

"I wanted to tell you," he said, his voice trailing off. He took a slug of his drink and wouldn't quite look her in the eye.

"Tell me what?"

"I stopped going. I met someone. A girl."

"Really," she said.

"Yeah. And, well, she's fantastic."

"You met a girl and she's fantastic."

"Yeah. I met her in the waiting room, actually. She was there to talk to one of the psychologists. Not as a patient. She wants to study counselling after her bachelor's, and her mom knew him, and, well, she was there when I came in and I met her. Manon." He looked at his mother and smiled. "I don't think I'm going to the psychologist any more."

"Call me but love and I'll be new-baptiz'd," Sandra said.

"Shakespeare, right? Manon loves Shakespeare. She's going to London in August to see a couple of his plays at the Globe Theatre. It's new, but they've tried as much as possible to make it like the original. Manon says its wicked."

Sandra doubted he had spoken this many pleasant words to her in a year. "You thinking of tagging along?"

"I'd like to," he said, looking away for a moment and then back at her. "I haven't asked her yet. I'm afraid she'll say no."

"Well," Sandra said. She smiled, stepping forward to put her arms around him. "That's wonderful, Dan." He felt so much larger than she remembered. She said, "Welcome to the adult world."

That August, Sandra rattled around the empty old house, living on her own for the first time in her life. Liam had left her, and she was exploring the dimensions of loneliness. It wasn't just Liam's abandonment that got to her, although that was a major part of it. Jillian was away, on a Mediterranean cruise for the entire month of August, with that new man she had taken up with. It was as though all her attachments to the planet were slowly dissolving – her family, her work.

She started waking regularly at three-thirty or four in the morning. She'd lie there, going over it all, wondering what was wrong with her, why she had behaved so badly to her husband and her son, what was it that made her always say too much or not enough. Sometimes, lying there, she had the curious sense she could levitate.

On the bright side, Dan was doing well. This girl Manon was ambitious, knew what she wanted, and pursued it full-bore. He would meet her in Europe for the last month of the summer. Liam had pulled some strings, but Dan would join Manon in Halifax that fall; he was going to start university.

She went to see her doctor. He gave her a prescription for sleeping pills, told her she'd had a shock and was in mourning for the loss of her marriage, that it might take some time to get over it. He added for good measure that it might also be menopause coming on and asked her to come back to see him in a month. He offered her antidepressants and the name of a therapist. She thanked him but refused.

Sandra tried to get involved in the new lab but found it a hard slog; she wondered if maybe she truly was too old to start over. Many of the people who worked at the institute had taken August off and she discovered she couldn't perform her experiments without technical help. Passing her old lab every day weighed on her, too. She began to feel a strange sort of disconnection, like she was going through the motions, a caricature of research, someone who didn't really care about the outcomes of her experiments one way or the other. Outside, the sky looked the wrong colour blue, the sun the wrong shade of yellow. At home, she discovered how much she hated to eat alone, and food gradually lost its appeal. She dropped fifteen pounds and became slow moving, sluggish, as though the air had become some more viscous fluid she moved through with difficulty. She spoke so little her voice began to feel rusty. By mid-August, her diabetes lab was finally history. She'd received a gold Seiko watch from the lab director at his retirement party. She never wore it. It sat in its box in a drawer, counting down the seconds.

She began to have the same dream over and over again, that she gradually became transparent until she finally floated away. She had to wonder: if she really did disappear, would it make any difference?

The late-August day was stifling, the midday sky almost white with heat. Through the windshield, the asphalt shimmered. Sandra concentrated on the road, aware she was hardly at her best. After ten days with almost no sleep, even walking a straight line would have been quite a challenge. She was certain she would fail just about every sobriety test except maybe the breathalyser. She negotiated the empty streets without incident; most people were probably still away on vacation.

Sandra parked the van in the lot of a familiar sculpture garden beside a lakeside bicycle path. She saw a man working to get a multicoloured kite aloft, running, switching back repeatedly, trying to scare up some wind. Must be too hot, Sandra thought. After a while he seemed to give up. He offered the kite to his little dark-haired girl, then flopped onto a red gingham spread where a woman sat amid the ruins of lunch. The toddler wandered, the kite dragging behind her as though she had sprung a tail.

Sandra pulled things from an old tote bag. As the air conditioning dissipated, the sides of the van seemed to press in on her. There was no note: she wasn't sure what to say, or to whom to address it. Why was she doing this? She had run out of steam. Liam had his own life. Dan too. He wasn't completely grown, true, but he didn't need her anymore, she had to face it. And for her? Her old life had vanished, and she just couldn't imagine herself into a new one. Sandra hoped neither of them would blame themselves but frankly was too tired to care, too tired to keep it all going, this pretence of a life, a life that had morphed somehow into a sentence to be served. She was tired, that was all. And she could no longer see that it mattered whether she was actually there or not.

On the upholstery beside her sat the vial of insulin she'd taken from her old lab and stored in her fridge the past few weeks, the syringes and needles in their shrouds of paper and plastic, a pill bottle with eight orange sleeping pills knocking around inside, just to take the edge off – she'd decided on insulin for the main event. It offered a certain symmetry she admired.

The new wallet she left in the tote bag. She had bought it only for the small card that read CONTACT IN CASE OF EMERGENCY and written her new boss's name and phone number on it. As someone who thought about suicide all the time, she figured he was the person least likely to be upset by the call, capable of identifying her and conveying the news. After all, how distressed could he be? He hardly knew her. The practicality of this decision satisfied her: at least she could still organize this. The wallet was small and black, not even real leather. Everything of value she'd left at home. She didn't want anyone taking her credit cards. She didn't want any more complications.

Just knock back the pills – she fished a bottle of water from the bag – slurp up some of the insulin, attach the 25-gauge needle to the syringe and away we go, she thought.

Not much to it, really. She popped open the pill bottle, and threw them into her mouth in several bursts, washing them down with tepid water. Overwhelmed suddenly by her own heartbeat and the closeness of the van – like a coffin she thought uneasily – she got out for a moment to calm herself.

She leaned her back against the van door, breathing deeply, face to the sun, eyes closed. In a bid to soothe her own agitation, she focused on the world around her. There was a small breeze after all, she found; the air steamed with humidity. She smelled the water in unpleasant, foul whiffs. She heard the gulls fighting over leftovers. Gradually she became aware of voices calling. They grew louder, then so insistent she reluctantly opened her eyes. It was the man and the woman from the picnic blanket. She watched as they tried to catch up to the little girl, still trailing the bedraggled red kite. The child skipped along the bike path, zigzagging, oblivious, dancing to some music only three-year-olds can hear. Then Sandra saw it, a fast-moving cyclist, an approaching blur in royal blue. The rest seemed to happen in slow motion. The cyclist swerved as if to avoid the child. The parents streamed toward their daughter, waving their arms, shouting, too far away to attract her attention. The child bopped along erratically, dragging her kite, until the bike smashed headlong into her, and then both she and the cyclist were briefly airborne and moving in opposite directions.

Sandra ran the short distance and dropped to her knees by the little girl who lay crumpled and unmoving, like a rag doll on an emerald rug. Carmine blood oozed from her ear. The parents arrived an instant later, looking as though they'd aged ten years. They appeared much too old to be responsible for such a young child. The mother stood wailing, hands on her cheeks. The father scooped the girl to him as Sandra tried her best to dissuade him, warning him her spine might be injured, some old first aid training returned to her in a wave.

Other people rushed over, cell phones plastered to their heads. Sandra felt herself elbowed to the periphery as the group buzzed like a disturbed hive. She looked away and spotted the cyclist, alone, splayed on his back on a grassy incline, and made her way over to him. His head moved from side to side. He moaned. Bloodied bone poked through the flesh of his right leg. His heel pointed skyward; Sandra was afraid to look at it too closely. She knelt on the grass beside him and asked if she could help.

"The girl," he said, finding her eyes with his. He looked sixteen or so, to Sandra's eyes impossibly young. "The little girl. I really hit her? She okay?"

"She's okay. Don't worry, she's fine, her parents are with her." Sandra's words all ran together as she prayed she was telling the truth. "Relax now, you must lie still. Someone is calling for help."

"I'm so cold," he choked out. He sobbed then and started to shake.

Sandra reached forward to unfasten his helmet, liberating a cascade of reddish curls. She stared at him for a moment, then reached forward to push the hair away from his eyes. "It's shock," she said. "You've hurt your leg and you're going into shock." Sandra felt drained and abruptly exhausted. She sat heavily on the grass and then lay down beside the young man, on his uninjured side. She took him in her arms. "Shh," she soothed, "it will be all right." He continued to cry and shake. Sandra felt the weight of the young man's body hold her firmly against the earth. She gazed up into the hazy blue sky. High above them the gulls floated freely.

He's just a boy, Sandra thought. Someone will have to take care of him. Someone will have to tell him it wasn't his fault.

SEA OF TRANQUILLITY

There's a quality to this silence that makes me think I should have faked it tonight.

Cal says into the darkness, "You okay, Hannah?"

"Yeah, don't worry about it," I say. "Must be the phase of the moon or something."

We face one another, feet touching in the middle of the bed, our bodies forming a misshapen heart. Each of us has the white sheet tucked under an arm.

"Hannah? You sure?"

"Yes," I answer, a shade too emphatic.

He reaches out and grazes my cheek with a finger.

I pull my head back, say goodnight, turn away. He moves closer, tucking under me until we're spooning. It isn't long before his breathing deepens and elongates, cresting like ocean waves.

I close my eyes, try to sleep, knowing very well I cannot. The clock reads 2:57 a.m. I reach for the small pill I left on the night table, just in case. It glows red in the light from the digital display; I've only recently figured out how to take it without water.

A neighbour's cat yowls. I picture the moon, lowering over the horizon. Cal turns, rustling the sheets. Tomorrow. Maybe tomorrow I'll tell him I'm leaving, if I can think of someplace to go. I've tried not to make a big deal of it, thought it was temporary, an erotic hiccup. But it's been a couple of months now since I've been able to come and I've taken it as a sign, promised myself I would leave if things didn't improve. There have to be consequences; what's missing is too basic, like the steel girders that hold a skyscraper upright. I can't just go on pretending nothing has changed.

At first, I did fake an orgasm or two, but of course, Cal noticed. And that hangdog look he gave me, well, *that* really had been beyond the limit. Surprising, really, given everything else I've managed to live through. It isn't anything Cal has done, or left undone, it's more like some primitive lizard-brain circuit has broken.

It isn't something I'm aware of having chosen.

Cal's a software engineer. On good days, he calls himself a code jock. We actually work at the same university, though in different departments, a coincidence we discovered that first night at the Lamplighters. He's short and chunky, with a dimple on his right cheek and wavy black hair. I usually find nail-biting a disgusting habit, but somehow, with Cal, I don't mind it so much.

Outside, it's silent as a sepulchre. Waiting for the pill to kick in, I crave distraction but it's the middle of the night. Then I remember the news today, that glimpse of the last of my childhood icons, the giant Guaranteed Pure Milk bottle. The mayor's decided it's got to go, after years spent rusting away, untended, the company defunct, in an area of downtown overdue for renewal. I've always loved it, this piece of genuine Montreal kitsch, propped up on scaffolding ten stories high. Tilted to the side as though just about to pour.

Every Tuesday and Thursday afternoon, when I was growing up, the Guaranteed Pure Milk Company would deposit two bottles, two percent butterfat, at the door of the upper duplex where we lived. And in the winter, when I returned home from school at the end of the day, glacial columns of milk would have pushed the white, green, and orange cardboard tops up and out from the glass bottles. My mother never seemed to remember to come down and get them.

In those days, my family took in foster kids. It was my mother's idea, like most that went on in my family. She'd read some heart-melting newspaper article about unwanted kids, and then talked and talked and talked till Dad finally said okay. He'd kick up a fuss sometimes but he ultimately agreed to just about anything she asked of him. The social worker showed up the very next day.

We weren't well off but my parents weren't in it for the money. In fact, I'm pretty sure we lost on the deal. We were always giving those kids more than the agency saw fit to provide. Like the time thirteen-year-old Colin wanted sealskin boots "like everybody else had." Sealskin boots were the kind of thing you just had to have, to fit in back in 1968.

Not that my parents indulged me that way. Like those white go-go boots I wanted – calf-high, zippers up the back finishing in large gold hoops. The agency paid for a foster kid's boots, sure, but not for *sealskin* boots, so my parents made up the difference. Maybe it was because they felt bad for the kid, having lost his family and all. Maybe they felt that the least they could do was make sure he got those boots. I hadn't really minded though, Colin getting his dream boots when I didn't get mine. Even then I recognized it was a fair enough trade. Maybe I have always been a little too accepting of whatever it was that fate dished out.

Two years now I've been with Cal, since a little after Molly died. I met him at a Lamplighters meeting, "support and self-help for bereaved parents." His marriage hadn't survived his son's passing, either. Four years old. Leukemia. Before it happened, I would have predicted that nothing could be more depressing than sitting in a room filled with grieving parents and grandparents, sometimes brothers and sisters, too. But I would have been wrong.

Before. Life had been perfect then, but I'd been too busy to notice, the universally fatal lapse. My daughter Molly was something special, not quite three, with a tiny, perfect rosebud mouth, a messy crown of chestnut curls, and a laugh that helped me finally understand the appeal of those feng shui waterfalls. Such a little thing, I never would've believed she could open that door off the kitchen.

She'd always been an early riser; it was a source of friction between Eric and me. We'd tried "Ferberizing" her, lying in the basement holding each other as she screamed her lungs out. But I couldn't follow through with it. I just didn't have the necessary ruthlessness to be that kind of parent. Several times, we consulted the pediatrician about Molly's sleep patterns, desperate for some strategy that would allow us, finally, to sleep past five-thirty in the blessed A-M. "Don't worry, she'll come round eventually," we'd be told as we sat there, bleary-eyed, while little Molly chirruped and gambolled.

That morning – I'll never forget it – I woke with a start. Glanced at the clock: 8:25. We hadn't slept in like that for months. Years, maybe. For a moment I luxuriated, stretching like a cat. I felt so good, like I might finally be in control of my life again. Car doors slammed, kids called out to one another on their way to school, and in the distance, a lawnmower started up. Sunlight sifted round the edges of the curtains, filling the room with a lemony glow. A cardinal was singing. Maybe Molly was settling down to a reasonable schedule, I thought. Finally. Had to happen sometime, didn't it? I rolled over and kissed Eric, snuggled a hand down, caressed him awake. "Good golly, Miss Molly," he whispered, smiling. We stayed there together another half hour or so, enjoying a little mental health day celebration.

I was the one who found her, floating, face down, just after 9:00 a.m. We'd had an above-ground pool installed earlier that spring. It was the only time she ever managed to get out of the crib on her own.

Cal turns over, tossing a leaden arm across me. I push it off, but gently. Shifting onto my back, I sigh. I try the deep, diaphragmatic breathing my therapist taught me, counting down, ten in, hold it one-two-three, ten out. I finish all ten breaths, but still there's a knot in my gut. I get up, go to the window, push the dusty curtains aside. The moon, its outline softened by clouds, floats like a fluorescent smear in the sky. I stare till I feel the chill, then pad across the hardwood and slip back into bed. I pinch the bridge of my nose with thumb and forefinger, screw my eyes tight, but I do not cry. Something else, there has to be something else.

When I was a kid, I walked to school and back, lunchtimes too. I'd meander, especially in the winter, take my time kicking through the slush at the edge of the street as I cleared a careful path for the snowmelt to reach the sewers. It left me feeling virtuous, even civic-minded. One Tuesday, I arrived home after one of my massive water diversion projects to find the milk bottles missing. I opened the door and slowly climbed the long, dark staircase. At the top, as usual, I kicked off my boots – my shoes remained stuck in their detested bottoms – and was gratified to hear them clunk their way down, hitting every step, coming to rest against the front door where my dad, as the next scheduled arrival, would have to push past them. But he never minded things like that, the things kids did that annoyed most grownups; he was good that way.

My socks shimmied half-off, I imagined myself as Godzilla stumping down the hallway toward the kitchen, sing-songing "Hi, Mom, I'm ho-ome." As though anyone could possibly have missed the commotion. Mom was in the kitchen, as usual, but with her was a little kid perched atop the Formica counter, hunched over as though trying to disappear. It offended me; we weren't allowed to sit up there. There was something about this kid, though, something that kept me from saying anything. The milk bottles glistened beside her, covered in rivulets of condensation.

Mom caught my eye. "The social worker brought them in," she said. She put a hand on the girl's head. "This is Cindy. She's going to stay with us awhile."

"Hey, Cin," I said, shrugging off my jacket and snow pants.

The kid bowed her head, then looked up at me, her eyebrows knitted together.

"Where will she sleep?" I shared a room with my sister and we were already pretty cramped.

"In a sleeping bag on the floor for tonight. We'll get bunk beds tomorrow, hopefully."

I figured the agency must have promised them. "Can I sleep on top?"

"We'll see, honey."

I couldn't take my eyes off this kid, there was something funny about her. Her mouth, it looked smudged somehow. The two halves didn't meet cleanly in the middle; one side looked as though it had been folded on top of the other and pressed in place.

"What's with her mouth?"

"She has cleft lip and palate. That means her lip and the roof of her mouth didn't form properly when she was growing in her mummy's tummy. But they've already operated on her once, and when she gets older, they'll fix it so you'd never know."

"How old are you anyway, Cindy?"

After a moment's silence, my mom answered for her: "She's five, but she looks quite a bit younger, don't you, sweetie?" She smoothed the girl's messy hair. "They said it was an emergency, that they couldn't leave her at home for one second longer."

The inflection in my mother's voice told me this was serious business. I looked Cindy over again – white baby shoes, a horizontally patterned jersey that snapped at the neck. She *was* awfully small, dressed more like a toddler than a kid who belonged in kindergarten. A diaper lurked beneath the grey corduroys. Her hair looked ratty, like it hadn't been washed in awhile. And she still hadn't uttered a word.

"Can't she talk?"

"Sure she can talk, she's just shy, that's all. Aren't you, Cindy?" My mom gave her a friendly squeeze but Cindy stiffened, snuffled loudly, and erupted in a phlegmy cough. Yuck, I thought, somebody better get this kid with the program.

"C'mon, Cindy," I said, picking her up and snuggling her onto my hip. I had younger cousins and was already an old hand at babysitting. "She can have my bed, Mom. I can sleep on the floor."

"Wanna walk," Cindy said, so I put her down. I felt a wisp of a hand slip into my own.

"I'll show you your new room – you're sharing with me and my sister. Do you know there's a full moon tonight? We'll go out later on and I'll show you, okay?"

Cindy wouldn't look at me but she nodded, putting her fingers in her mouth. It looked like she wanted to jam her whole hand in there.

A few weeks before Molly died, we'd decided we were ready for another baby. After the drowning, Eric honed in on that baby like a man wandering the desert who glimpsed a shimmering oasis. But I couldn't go through with it. I just knew it, the way you know about gravity before anyone's ever explained it. And nothing Eric said could change my mind; he was starting to seem more and more like a mirage to me anyway at that point, and so was our marriage – hazy, indistinct, maybe not even really there. When I finally told him how I felt, that I'd secretly gone back on the pill, the light leaked out of his eyes completely. That night, he packed and left. I wasn't sorry, exactly. Anyway, I'd studied physics. His leaving was inevitable, like a Newtonian principle: for every action, an equal and opposite reaction.

Soon as I could, I went back to work. Medical research. As a student, it seemed so altruistic but, in practice, it came down to decapitating mice and fishing out their intestines for molecular transport experiments. It took a lot of concentration and a lot of equipment: cages, balances, water baths, shakers, flasks, growth medium, test tubes and pipettes, alcohol, dry ice, a round fluorescent magnifying loop with a hinged arm, a miniature guillotine of stainless steel, scalpels, and a host of other sharp instruments. I was relieved to lose myself in something so absorbing, grateful not to have too many of my own neurons floating around, underused. And a couple of nights a week, I went to Lamplighter meetings in musty church basements all over Montreal. The group never forced people to tell their stories, or even to talk at all. A person could just sit there all night, listening, swallowing a scalding liquid that tasted more like melted brown crayons than coffee, so that's what I did. I never cried. I just tried to make sure I never went home alone to my empty house. The pool had been done away with even before Molly's funeral; somebody's brother-in-law took it down, I think. I was pretty doped up; the details are mercifully obscure.

Since Molly's death, Cal's the only one who's been able to make me feel much of anything. I have no idea why; he doesn't seem much different from any of the others I've brought home. But every once in a while when he touches me, I get the feeling, even if for the briefest instant, that maybe my life hasn't already ended, that maybe the future is still possible.

Cindy bloomed in our family circle, her baby shoes soon traded up for classic red leather Mary Janes. One spring morning, we both woke early. When I checked, Cindy's diaper was dry, so we rigged up the toilet seat insert and she gave it a go. The smile on that kid's face as she heard her own tinkles was so broad, it looked like her upper lip might tear right apart again. I found a pair of honeycomb-quilted training pants in a bureau drawer and told her she was a big girl now. "You can wear underwear, just like everybody else. No more diapers."

I was as proud as she was.

Then, one night, my mom went to the movies with a friend, leaving Dad to take care of us girls. At bedtime, he scooped little Cindy up, tucking her under one arm. "Let's read *Goodnight Moon,*" he said. "Okay, young lady?"

"No," Cindy answered in a tiny voice, struggling a little in his arms. "Let me go," she whispered. Either he didn't hear her or he didn't get it, I was never sure which. Maybe he thought she just didn't want to go to bed; I've always had the feeling dads could be kind of dense.

"Let me *go,*" Cindy repeated.

My dad kept on walking toward the bedroom, whistling, oblivious, till Cindy threw up. At first, we thought it was a virus or something, but it kept happening, until we noticed it was only when my dad tried to do something with her. Then came the day he put Cindy on his lap to tie her shoelaces. Cindy wet her pants. After six months without any diapers. Mom called the social worker and forced the truth out of her. Something had happened between Cindy and her father, though I was never told what, exactly. I just got a long lecture from my mom: about not talking to strangers, especially strange men, about never leaving Cindy alone outside.

Another day, not long after, I rounded the corner just in time to see a police car peeling away from the curb in front of our house. It was the first time I ever felt my heart fall. I just stood there for a moment, then ran the rest of the way home, my throat tight, my head pounding. My mom was seated in the rocking chair, wiping her own tears away and trying to comfort Cindy who, howling, inconsolable, was sitting on my mom's lap. Cindy's father had shown up to bellow and rage at the front door, his fury echoing, amplifying their terror, as it mounted the long, dark staircase. The police had taken him away.

After that, I spent even more time with the kid, talking, reading stories, teaching her to play jacks and other simple games with cards or a ball, things any normal five-year-old girl could do. It was 1969, men were going to the moon, and the infinite universe – the sky, the planets and stars – became my new passion. For the science fair, I was making a model solar system: covering foam balls with papier mâché, painting them, rigging little motors that spun them round their axes. I let Cindy help. My project made the finals in the regional competition and this so impressed my parents that they gave me a small telescope to mark the occasion. We'd pass evenings gazing at the stars and the moon, trying to locate the Sea of Tranquillity. I taught Cindy to recognize the Big Dipper, that the sun was a giant ball of fire.

Cal's dreaming. "No. *No*," he says. Then something I can't catch, something not quite words. He's too close now, making me feel too warm. I try to put more distance between us. As if that's possible. Cal's a good man. Has a stutter his parents spent thousands trying to correct. He told me it only shows up when he is tired or stressed, which, when I think about it, should be all the time, at least since I've known him. But maybe after the worst happens – the thing you can't even imagine – you relax, sort of. Maybe there's a version of freedom that comes with being pre-disastered.

We don't talk much. I've heard him describe those twin deaths, his son and his marriage. I've felt him inside me. What more do I need to know? It had been enough that he was gentle, that he was here. Not much of a life between us, but for a while there it seemed like it might be enough for me, an acceptable form of limbo. Or is that purgatory? My theology's a little rusty.

How naïve the young are, how complacent, believing that they deserve success, their good fortune, because they're good people, doing everything right. That when bad things happen, it's just karma, because "what goes around comes around." Positively Old Testament, isn't it, an eye for an eye and all that? Amazing, really, that anyone can still see at all. Nothing more than a shared delusion, the idea there's any justice in this universe. There isn't. I know. I've looked for it everywhere.

The waif with dirty hair and baby clothes grew six inches and gained eleven pounds in the short time she'd been with us. The social worker announced herself pleased. Cindy was doing well in kindergarten, reading even. And we'd become inseparable. I was closer to that kid than I'd ever been to my "real" sister, closer than I would be to anyone else, ever. And that, I know, was the original sin.

Early summer, Sunday, late afternoon. The two of us begged to go to the park before dinner. It was a languid day; the house smelled of onions and brisket and apple cake. My mom didn't want us to go, but our chores were done, I pointed out, and my homework. I was pretty relentless, and she finally gave in, telling me to take my watch, to be home for 6:30.

At the park, we threw ourselves into it, climbing the jungle gym (though I was afraid of heights), making mud pies in the sandbox, tumbling down a grassy slope over and over again, laughing. Everything was lush, green and blooming, full of possibility. School was almost over; I was teaching Cindy the chant "No more pencils, no more books, no more teacher's dirty looks." She giggled every time she said it; she loved being naughty. I could have sworn there was perfection in the slant of the light as the day began to fade. We were on the swings, a persimmon smudge in the sky.

"Six-thirty, kid, time to go," I said.

"Can't we touch the moon, Hannah, just once more? Pretty please?"

Sometimes a sliver of moon appeared in the sky, and we'd imagine that if we went high enough, we could sail into space and be the first girls in history to set foot on the moon. It was irresistible, our secret fantasy, and so I gave in, in love with my role as the indulgent older sister even though I knew we should be leaving. Then Cindy asked if we could swing together, instead of side-by-side, so I put her on my lap, holding her close. Cindy in my right hand, the swing in my left, I flew through space, hair streaming, legs pumping.

"Higher," Cindy shouted, "higher."

And there we were, stretching, stretching, doing our damnedest to touch the moon. Cindy squealed in delight, and suddenly we were pivoting, slipping backward, tumbling down to earth. I fought to stay upright, to keep hold of the swing, to make sure that if anyone hit the dirt it would be me alone, that Cindy would only thump harmlessly against me. And in that, at least, I was successful.

I lay flat on my back, dust rising, gobsmacked. The swing jangled against the metal post, seemingly miles above me. Cindy was crying, my head hurt, my back hurt, my *everything* hurt; I may even have passed out for a moment. The swing set looked bizarre, strangely distant, like the walls did when I had a fever or lay in bed late at night, overexcited about something and unable to sleep. Winded, I struggled to catch my breath. And then from an eternity above us, from so far away they might have come from outer space, two arms reached down and pulled Cindy from my clasp. And even though I'd never seen him before,

I knew it was her father. We were two young girls, alone and vulnerable.

I've told myself every day since then that there wasn't a thing I could do about it. But I will always know the truth: I should have tried harder. I should never have let her go.

Five in the morning. The sun might be rising but I do my best not to acknowledge it.

Anorgasmia – I looked it up – can be primary or secondary. More frequent in women than men, it's often caused by antidepressants, sexual inhibition, or sexual trauma. Not quite the end of the world, as I well know, having lived more than once through the end of the world.

Cal rolls toward me, reaches out and curls round me and, just like that, we're spooning again. "Enough tossing and turning," he says, "we're on the way back, you know we are." He murmurs this into the nape of my neck, kissing me there as though sealing a promise; it makes me shiver. "Just let's stop lying to each other," he says.

And suddenly the whole thing – what he's said and the way he's said it, the kiss, the shiver, this whole long night – resonates somewhere inside me, like tumblers turning in a lock. Then I feel it – sleep staking its claim, moving through my bloodstream, merciful, like forgiveness, flowing from wherever it's been sequestered all this time. And all at once, it's so easy, falling asleep, like slipping away in the clear blue sky, like sliding beneath still waters. And I realize that maybe I shouldn't leave Cal just yet, that maybe there is something between us. That even the smallest bit of something is worth more than a whole lot of nothing.

In the weeks right after she disappeared, we did get several phone calls from Cindy, crying and saying she missed us. Cindy's father must have dialled for her, trying to calm her down maybe, or trying to drive us all crazy, who understands such people? It just about killed my mother; cured her forever of foster kids.

A couple of years later, at breakfast one morning, Mom let out a cry and dropped the container of milk she'd been holding. She just stood there, one hand covering her mouth. I thought she was horrified by the mess spreading across the linoleum, but it was Cindy's photo she was looking at, there on the milk carton, under the caption MISSING. They never did find her, not even a trace.

For years afterwards, I'd lie outside on summer nights with my telescope and aim for Tranquillity. I'd trace the Big Dipper and stare at the cold-hot stars, wondering where Cindy was. Imagining – praying? – the kid was somehow safe and loved, that maybe she was gazing up at the selfsame sky.

Thinking of, remembering, someone like me.

CHERYL

Look what I found in this stupid magazine. I mean, can you believe this shit? This is just like one of those courses my psychiatrist keeps telling me to take. "Awkward at parties or other social occasions? If you're not living your best life, if your nerves suck the fun out of everything, these ten tips will help you stop blushing and enjoy life to the max!"

What a steaming pile of crap. As if, after forty-three years of never having anyone to talk to, of nobody giving a shit, I could just take a course, have someone make me over, have them turn my life around. As if it's so easy to just decide, "Okay, Cher, just a few exercises here, hold hands, sing a couple of rounds of 'Kumbaya' and presto change-o! Everything'll just be okaaay!"

As if happiness is some kind of post-hypnotic suggestion.

I've tried hypnosis, you know. A bunch of years ago now, with my first psychiatrist. I'd see him every couple of weeks. He said I was depressed, started me on these pills, antidepressants. Prozac, Zoloft, Mannerix, Celexa, and on and on and on. Whenever I came in he'd say, "How are you doing today, Cher?" And I'd tell him I was still thinking about it.

Killing myself.

Not that I wanted to, you understand. But I had these thoughts. I'd walk out on the balcony, and they'd just pop into my head. I couldn't control them, they'd just come, you understand? They said jump, jump, JUMP!

Or in the kitchen where I work, at the daycare? I pick up the lunch and bring it to the kids, and sometimes they have these knives out, these cleavers they have. Huge blades, glinting in the light. Sometimes I swear they were winking at me, in some sort of secret code. Other times, I'd hear voices saying these knives would be just right. For cutting myself.

God, I hate when that happens.

He used to change my medication, every single appointment. The dosage first, then when that didn't work, he'd try a new drug. The doctor I have now says you just don't do that, it takes six weeks at least to know if something's working, maybe more. I don't know why he kept changing it, that first one. I didn't know any better. I just felt so terrible, you know? I couldn't sleep, I heard voices, the light off the knives flashing at me... He tried five or six different medications, different combinations. He'd say take more of this one, take less of that. And then one day he said, "We could try hypnosis."

And I would have done anything by then, you understand? If he'd said, "Just hit your thumb with this hammer," I would have. Absolutely. Because nobody wants to feel this way.

So he'd fiddle with prescriptions for a while, then tell me to lie down on this couch he had. Brown leather, real uncomfortable, made me sweat. "Relax," he'd say, "just relax. Think of the most beautiful place you've ever been, imagine yourself back there." And I remembered this meadow we used to go to, my family. For picnics. With wild flowers and long grass, the kind of field you see in commercials. The woman at one end, the man at the other and they run to each other in slow motion, her long blonde hair flowing like water, and they meet in the middle, both of them smiling like fiends, and she jumps in his arms and he lifts her, her dress swirls, she throws her head back and laughs and then slides down and they kiss…

I've been kissed a few times, you know. Don't laugh, I didn't always look this way. I wasn't so bad when I was at university. I flunked out, of course. I had learning disabilities as a kid, okay? I was in special classes all through school, three elementary schools and three different high schools. Because we moved a lot. There was always something wrong with the places we rented. The landlord would promise to paint, maybe. And then he wouldn't and my dad would get mad and we'd move. One time, my brother's playing hockey in the driveway got everyone bent out of shape. The noise, the marks on the garage door, some people are just maniacs about stuff like that. Once we moved just across the street but it put us in a different school district and no matter what my mother did, I had to transfer. I mean, we just moved across the fucking street, for God's sake!

After high school I went to junior college at the New School. There were no real marks there, it was all self-evaluation, group evaluation. The teachers told me, "You can do anything here, Cher. Be what you want to be, do what you want to do. You only have to try. Only believe." Man, did I fall for that shit, like a ton of bricks. I believed. I wished. I tried. It was like living in a Disney movie, I kid you not. Close your eyes, tap your heels, and whisper, "There's no place like home, there's no place like home."

I got great grades at the New School, for the first time in my entire fucking life. They told me whatever held me back in the past, that was all over now. They didn't say presto change-o but they might just as well have. When I graduated, they gave me a prize for being the most self-actualized student, can you believe that? I mean, can you fucking believe that? They called it the Beaver Award. Ha. I should've known, with a name like that, what a crock it was. Okay, so it's our national animal, but still, how stupid is that? The Beaver Award. I should've known. Instead, I felt good, I felt loved, I felt... cured. For the first time in my life, I belonged. I thought, why not? Why couldn't I get better? Miracles happen. Growth.

So that was how I wound up going to university. And not just a university here in Montreal – we have four of them, eh, two are even English – no, by that point I was convinced I could go anywhere, do anything. So I went far from home, for the first time ever, for university. And when I was there, I met some boys, I got kissed, I learned to drink Purple Jesus and slurp electric jello. And then, when it all fell apart – I was failing courses and the counselor told me I belonged in a program for disabled students, when I finally crashed and started screaming that I wanted to die – they just called my mother and she came on the train and packed up my stuff and brought me home.

I was in a bad way then. I lay in bed in the dark for weeks. I couldn't have gotten up for anything, not even if you paid me.

It wasn't the first time I'd been sick because of school.

As a kid, I missed a lot of school because of stomach aches. My mother took me from doctor to doctor. After awhile, the doctors decided there was nothing wrong with my stomach. They finally told my mother I was malingering.

Malingering. Sounds devilish, doesn't it?

Malingering. They said I was imagining the pains in my stomach. But I didn't have such a good imagination in those days. I do now, though. It's the drugs, I think.

And the electric shock.

I found out about electric shock through Anna, a woman I met at the depression group on Monday nights. Anna told me nothing had ever worked for her like electric shock. So I asked my doctor. She said she didn't believe in it, that she only used it as a last resort, when nothing else worked.

Fast-forward a few more years.

I've been in the hospital five or six more times and now none of the drugs do any good. One of the doctors on the psych ward finally talks my psychiatrist into trying electric shock. And it works!

At least, I haven't been back in thc hospital since. Every four weeks I get it, like clockwork. The only thing is, it scrambles me a little. My mind, it jumps from thing to thing. I forget a lot, too. How to get places when I drive. The past. A lot of it's gone. My sister asks me something about sleep-away camp and I have to confess, I can't remember. On the other hand, sometimes I just sit back and watch the stories unwind in my head. It's like I've got a TV up there. Like I'm at the goddamn movies.

One time, I went to Anna's house. And she told me she had to take a nap – the meds'll do that to you. Sometimes they feel like fifty-pound sacks of cement on your back, dragging you down, practically knocking you over. But if you complain to the doctor about it, he just says, "That's not the medication, that's the depression."

The de-pre-ssion!

Sometimes I think doctors haven't got a clue. Not the faintest. Sometimes I think they're all full of shit. Fifty-pound sacks of it.

Like that hypnosis doctor I was talking about? He tells me to close my eyes and imagine this couple running across that field – like a commercial for hair dye or something, I kid you not – and the kissing and the next thing, I realize, it's him. The hypnosis doctor. He's kissing me and touching my breasts, he really had this thing about massaging my big mushy breasts. He slides his hand between my legs and his tongue's in my mouth and it feels so good, the lovely sunny meadow, being naked in the sun, so warm, I was sweating…

I went to that guy for two more years, two *years* of paying under the table for "hypnosis." Two years of paying him to have sex with me, can you believe it?

I mean *can you fucking believe that?*

The psychiatrist I'm seeing now doesn't. She says what I'm describing is called transference. She says I just imagined I was in love with him, just imagined he was touching me. Just *imagined* having sex with him. She can't imagine he was actually having sex with me but she has no problem imagining I have such a good imagination.

Imagine that, eh?

Transference. I swear, these educated assholes have a word for everything, they've got an excuse for ab-so-lutely everything!

Nothing is ever their fault.

I never had much of an imagination before. But now, well, between the drugs and the electric shock, it's like I've got a fucking satellite up there, I swear to God.

Like that time I was at Anna's and she went to take a nap? She goes to her bedroom for awhile and I just sat there on the couch. And I start seeing things. In my head. Imagining. Malingering. Later on, I call up my sister – she's a writer – and I say, "Have I got a story for you!" She says okay, tell me.

I'm not sure she really wants to hear it.

Okay, now I'm just messing with you. I *know* she doesn't want to hear it. Because she hates talking to me, absolutely fucking *hates it*!

But she has to listen to me sometimes, doesn't she? She's my sister, after all, she's supposed to love me, she's supposed to take an interest, help take care of me. So sometimes she just has to.

Oh, I try not to call her too often. But you have to speak to somebody every once in a while, don't you? Or you'll go mad.

That's funny, isn't it? Goddamn. I kid you not.

I've told her about the light flashing off the knives at the daycare, I've told her about the voices and the balcony. I never mentioned the faces on the floor, the ones that talk to me. I'm not completely heartless. These faces just appear and tell me what a stupid cow I am, how ugly and worthless. How much better off everyone would be if I was dead. Daring me.

But I just can't do it, I can't, you understand? Oh, I know I should, it'd be best for everyone, really. But I'm too much of a coward.

They hate me most of all for that, the voices. I've taken a few pills in the past, enough to take the edge off, knock me out. Enough to get me admitted, my stomach pumped and all that. They don't really pump it, eh? They just make you drink this liquid charcoal stuff. Black as sin. Why *that* stuff doesn't kill you, I have no fucking idea.

I don't even remember the story I imagined, waiting for Anna to get up from her nap. Just that when I got to the point with the gang rape – four guys holding me down, taking turns, sticking themselves in me every which way – my sister stops me. Sorry, she says, she can't listen to any more of this. It's too upsetting.

Up-sett-ing!

Like, I'm not the only coward in this relationship.

Like, I'm not the only one who doesn't want to see these movies in her head, or hear these voices. But unlike my fucking sister, I can't just hang up the phone on them, can I? Unlike my fucking cunt of a fucking sister, I'm stuck with this fucking satellite in my head.

I don't know why I'm telling you all this. Because the reason they sent me here has nothing to do with Anna or my sister or either of my stupid psychiatrists, the one who fucked me or the one who doesn't believe me. I just got distracted by that stupid magazine.

It's because of that David, isn't it? What I did.

David came to the class I worked with in September. Four years old, but he never really knew *what* was going on. Couldn't learn the words to any of the stupid songs they tried to teach him, couldn't seem to learn to tie his shoes. Never remembered the way back to class from the bathroom. Couldn't zip his own jacket, for fuck's sake. And the other kids, they noticed. They may be four and five years old but they're sharp as tacks, really. And David... well, he wasn't. So they attacked him, those sharp tacks, vicious attacks. Teased him, poked him when they thought no one was looking. They'd trip him or take his toys away, grab the dessert right out of his hands. Apple slices, granola bars, whatever.

He's a sweet little boy, really. Loves anything to do with cars. And I was real soft on him. You're not supposed to have favourites at the daycare, see, but everyone plays favourites there, all the fucking time. But none of the teachers wanted David, so he became my pet. Eventually, I realized he reminded me of the way the other kids treated me when I was a kid. When they weren't completely ignoring me, that is.

I'm still not sure which is worse.

David was four, supposedly, but he really looked more like a two-year-old. So this morning, he's so busy playing with that little Fisher Price garage they have, he forgets about going to the bathroom and… he wets himself.

He stands and there's this puddle under him, his pants are dark with a wetness you just can't ignore. And the other kids start calling him names, "baby" and "retard." Oh, it was awful. And Mireille, the teacher in the room – I'm there bringing up the snacks, and she has twenty kids to take care of – Mireille sees me and says, "Cher, thank goodness! Can you take David to the washroom and clean him up, change his clothes?" The kids all have a change of clothes there. The daycare director insists we change the kids' clothes at the end of the day so they go home clean – she's a demon about the kids looking clean for their parents, like being clean is so fucking important. Goddamn, that I just don't get. And I liked this boy, this David who reminded me of me, so I said… yes.

Yes, I would take him to the bathroom and clean him up, I would take care of him, yes.

But David kept on crying, he just would *not* stop crying. Even after I told him it was okay, it wasn't his fault, it didn't matter. And I was holding him, crying with him, I just felt so bad. For him. For me.

And suddenly, it started.

The imagining.

I could see how it would always be. Nothing working out, even when he tried his hardest. People making fun of him. Being lonely, all alone, all the time, no matter where he went. It would be awful, it would be awful for him his entire life.

I didn't mean to, don't you see? It was just an accident. A terrible, terrible accident. But you have to admit, he's better off now than he was before. Better off than I am. Better not to grow up. At least he isn't suffering anymore.

I picked him up, this poor sad little boy, this hopeless useless little crying boy. No one understood him, no one would ever love him. The faces there on the floor, they were whispering. David crying. He was so small.

I was soothing him, you understand?

I held him tight against my chest, my big mushy breasts. And the voices kept whispering. And they mentioned those knives. And I hugged him even tighter then and I shouted back at them, "No way, there's no goddamn way, would you just shut up, you malingering demons, would you just *shut the fuck up*?"

We sat there together for a while and I rocked him, I shushed him. And then I thought… I imagined… he'd finally calmed down. At last. Little David. He was feeling better. So I tried to sit him up but, *oh God*, he was all limp, he was like a rag doll. He was dead.

I smoothed the hair from his forehead, very, very gently. And I kissed him on the lips. Because no one should die without having been really kissed on the lips.

I told him I was glad for him, that at least no one could hurt him anymore. And I mean it.

And you'll never get me to take that back, okay? Uh-uh, no way.

Never.

THE WOMAN WITH DEADLY HANDS

There once was a woman whose hands killed whatever they touched. It wasn't something she did on purpose – it was just something her hands did, outside her control. But it distressed her greatly, and as a result she kept to herself mostly, afraid she might accidentally touch someone at dinner while passing the rolls, say, or at a party.

Of course, she was an orphan. She wound up in institutional care after hugging her parents, one after the other, on her sixth birthday (this was how she first found out about her hands). The coroner ruled her parents died of heart attacks within minutes of each other, a freakish coincidence, the sort of story that encourages romantics to believe in true love.

The girl wanted to make sense of what had happened but she couldn't remember much of it. Her parents had given her a stack of new books for her birthday – a collection of short novels by Roald Dahl. Her favourite had been *Matilda*. In fact, this was the first book she could recall having read completely on her own, and she'd started it that very night. She remembered the birthday candles flickering atop the cake and, that night, the book, the tented sheet and flashlight. Try as she might, what happened next was a mystery, though the horrible truth – that she was a murderer – remained all too clear. The girl grew to be a woman, hugging to herself her lonely deep, dark secret.

At eighteen, she gained possession of her parents' cottage and all their belongings – paintings, ceramic eggcups and silver-plated spoons inscribed with the names of cities and countries. But her parents' most beloved possessions had been their books. The woman loved books, too – reading had illuminated the lonely fog of her institutional life (no worries about hugging there). Growing up, she had spent all her spare time reading, hours and hours each and every day. Reading became a form of meditation for her, the torrent of words helping her keep sad reality at bay.

The woman made numerous additions to her parents' literary collection, until even the kitchen and laundry room were overrun. Paperbacks gathered dust on tables and counters, *In Search of Lost Time* lurked under her bed, signed first editions teetered in towers on staircases or in stacks beside chairs. Some years she'd make a game of it, reading only Turkish authors, say, the next year only Nobel Prize winners. The year she attempted to limit her reading to Turkish Nobel Prize winners she was forced to abandon the enterprise when she discovered there were too few of them. The woman considered books her salvation. In this instance, as in others, she may have been somewhat deluded.

The woman's cottage had a green lawn and a white picket fence. She tried many times to put in a flower garden, with predictable results, with results that made her weep because she loved flowers so. She contented herself instead with a perfect lawn, fertilized, watered, and cut in such a way that it did not suffer from her affliction.

Next door lived two men that the woman, like others in town, called the Bloom brothers, though everyone knew deep down they weren't brothers at all. It was just easier to call them brothers than to accept there might be another reason two grown men would spend their lives together. Over time, the Bloom brothers resembled each other more and more – their hair went from auburn and black to grey, the one with the thick mane started losing it, the tall one grew more stooped. The townspeople sighed with relief because this made the lies they had told themselves feel more like the truth.

The woman would wave to the Blooms when she saw them and comment often on their wonderful flowers – nasturtiums spilling from painted buckets, profusions of peonies, Japanese irises of royal purple, Solomon's seal, bleeding hearts, meandering clematis, and an immense rambling rose bush, red, on a trellis by the front stairs.

The Bloom brothers eventually noticed that, though friendly, their neighbour would never shake either of their hands, and it rankled. Was this some subtle homophobia, they wondered? They discussed it at least weekly in the summer, when they met her most often. These conversations usually occurred over dinner on their deck, which they called (each admitting its pretension to himself but never to the other) the terrace. Gauze curtains billowed from the sliding doors, tiny icicle lights extended in an intentional tangle along banisters, and the Blooms drank litres of red wine as they talked and ate a variety of foods – steaks or sausages, say, or chops, chicken brochettes, filet mignon, sometimes fish, along with red, green, and orange peppers, thick slices of eggplant (arguing about whether to salt them before grilling became a kind of ritual), zucchini, and red onion, the vegetables brushed with balsamic vinaigrette and sprinkled with rosemary (of which the tall, thin, bald Bloom disapproved because rosemary got stuck between his teeth, but he endured it for the sake of conjugal harmony). The shorter, balder Mr. Bloom wore a white apron like a butcher's while he grilled. Each carried a huge half-filled, stemmed balloon glass, convinced red wine was good for him (and imbibing a little too much of it!).

The Blooms experimented with the woman next door, plumbing the dimensions of her aversion to them (their words), showing up at her door to say her paper had mistakenly landed on their grass, offering her coupons from the one newspaper she didn't subscribe to, surprising her with flowers from their garden (these she enjoyed for days because they were already dead when she got them).

"I brought her a blueberry pie this morning, and she smiled and seemed genuinely happy to have it, but when I tried to hand it to her—"

"She asked you to come in and leave it on her kitchen table, am I right?" Jake said.

Gary, the balder Mr. Bloom, turned the steaks, saying "Mm-hmm" into his wineglass.

Jake, laying the silverware, said, "She's pulled that one on me many times."

"We should do something about it, we really should."

"You've been saying that for five years now."

"This time I mean it."

"Like what?"

"We could take her to the Civic Relations Board."

"Isn't that a little extreme? Other than this one small thing, she's always been exceedingly pleasant."

"This entire situation is beginning to affect my sleep," said the shorter Mr. Bloom, whose sleep was delicate and another matter of some discussion.

Jake, the taller Mr. Bloom, thought any sleep problem more likely related to the amount of wine Gary (the shorter Mr. Bloom) consumed, but he knew better than to mention this. He pursed his lips and returned to the kitchen for plates and a platter.

"Well?" Gary was using great burnished tongs to remove food from the grill.

"The process is already underway, I suppose. Am I right?"

Gary handed over the laden platter, and hung the tongs on the side of the barbeque. Raising his wineglass, he said with a smile, "Jake, you are always right."

So that's how it was that the woman whose hands killed whatever they touched was summoned several weeks later to a hearing of the Civic Relations Board. She was shocked and chagrined by the official letter, as much by the notion that the Bloom brothers thought she disapproved of them as by the dread that she might have to reveal her deep, dark secret. In the period before the hearing, she hid behind her curtains till the Blooms left every morning, mortified at the idea of having to talk to them.

On the appointed day, she called in sick – she was a medical transcriptionist – and took the bus downtown, while the Blooms drove their air-conditioned Ford Escape hybrid, the colour of a school bus. In the waiting area the woman and the Blooms acknowledged one another, and then quickly hid behind magazines.

Ultimately, they were ushered into an office with a large oval table. On it rested a tray with a carafe and six over-turned glasses. The walls were covered with posters of smiling children, while a floor-to-ceiling window provided a soothing view of the town and the river and the mountains beyond. On either side of the window stood a large potted plant.

"Maître Louis Robichaud," said the Civic Relations Board commissioner, putting out his hand. He was about the woman's age, in a black tie, white shirt, and charcoal bespoke suit. His hair was oiled, combed back from a high forehead over black eyes and an aquiline nose. He explained this would be an exploratory meeting. The Blooms introduced themselves, shook Robichaud's hand, and sat down. The woman smiled, telling him her name but holding her hands at her sides. Jake gave Gary a significant look. The woman sat across from the Blooms.

There was a pain in her chest she was doing her best to ignore.

Maître Robichaud sat at the end of the table. He had worked for the United Nations in conflict resolution and confidence-building, he informed them, glancing at each of them in turn. "We have four rules in this office. First – and this is my absolute, number one, cardinal rule – always speak civilly to one another. Second, never interrupt the person who is speaking. Third, always tell the truth. And fourth, you must truly want to solve the conflict. If you can agree to these rules, I am confident we can solve the problem, right here, just the four of us."

Everyone agreed to the rules. "Great," said Robichaud (who had a lunch date forty-five minutes hence).

"These rules," Jake asked, "do they come from the UN?"

The woman heard something in Maître Robichaud's laugh that reminded her of small bells. "Actually, they come from my ten-year-old nephew. He learned them in peer mediation at middle school."

Gary flushed.

Maître Robichaud perused the papers before him and recounted the complaint. Jake nodded; Gary cleared his throat, saying Robichaud had got it just right. Maître Robichaud turned to the woman. "And your position, Madame?"

"There's been a terrible misunderstanding," she said, talking to her lap. "I never meant any disrespect." She looked up and noticed Maître Robichaud's five o'clock shadow. Though he resembled an undertaker, she still found him handsome. Of course, this made everything worse.

"I have nothing against the Blooms. They keep their house well. I often tell them how much I admire their garden. I brought them some winc from a tour I took to Niagara last summer. I always thought we got along well." Her voice grew lower and lower until the three men strained to hear her.

Jake shifted in his seat, Gary grew pinker still. The woman smiled, looking miserable.

"That's all very well but it hardly explains why she refuses to touch us," Gary said.

"And if she shook your hands right now, would that end all this?"

The Blooms regarded each other. "Yes, I think so," Gary Bloom said.

"Then it's settled." Maître Robichaud rose and glanced at his watch (his reservation was at a very good restaurant: they would neither seat an incomplete party nor hold the table longer than ten minutes).

"I'm sorry," the woman said, "but I cannot shake their hands."

Gary said, "You see what we have to put up with?"

The woman sighed. "Well, then," she said. She rose and went over to the *Ficus benjamina* by the window, touching it with an outstretched index finger in the manner of God approaching Adam on the ceiling of the Sistine Chapel. Like a study in time-lapse photography, the leaves crisped up and drifted to the carpet.

For a moment, only the rattle of the ventilation system was audible.

"That happens to those plants all the time," Gary said.

The woman went silently to the dark-leaved rubber plant, touching it, too. Those leaves also dried out and fell. In the ensuing silence, she seemed to glide back to her seat.

"I used to polish that plant's leaves myself," Maître Robichaud said.

Gary Bloom said, "You mean…"

The woman nodded.

Gary turned to his partner and said, "Right again." Jake, to his credit, said nothing.

The Blooms withdrew their complaint, promising never to reveal the woman's infirmity, and she apologized for hurting their feelings.

"Don't even think it," Gary said.

Maître Robichaud announced his report would not mention the woman's hands.

Over the next several weeks, the woman sat home reading full-time, the Blooms occasionally attempting to invite her to dinner, or offering her another pie, to no avail. The Blooms began caring for her lawn – "It's the least we can do," Gary told her answering machine. The woman was down to eating saltines from the back of the pantry, and old tins of smoked oysters. She didn't care what she ate; she was hardly hungry anymore, anyway.

The Blooms sat on their terrace, drinking more than ever, gloomily fretting as sundown arrived earlier each evening. Finally, after weeks of despond, they phoned Maître Robichaud; if he couldn't help, they would request a mental health assessment for the woman. After all, they knew she had no one else.

Next evening, Maître Robichaud arrived with two brown grocery bags, a baguette under one arm. The woman, her appetite resurrected by the scent of barbequed chicken, surprised herself by admitting him. (While Maître Robichaud and the woman spoke in her doorway, Jake found Gary twitching the living room sheers, peering through a set of field glasses. The Blooms proceeded to have their first real argument in years.)

In the kitchen, Maître Robichaud unpacked a nine-inch potted azalea (fuchsia), three oranges, bottles of olive oil and balsamic vinegar, the chicken in a domed plastic container and a pair of what looked like grey oven mitts. Maître Robichaud told her to sit while he fetched plates and cutlery. He filled glasses with tap water, sliced the oranges (six wedges each), and swirled the vinegar into the oil on a plate. The woman fell on the food with her hands. They ate without speaking, dipping hunks of baguette in the savoury liquid. Maître Robichaud ate little. Mostly, he sat back and watched.

When they had finished, they washed, one at a time, at the kitchen sink. He told the woman to put on the gloves and touch the plant.

She said, "I've tried gloves before."

"Not these," he said.

She did as he suggested. The plant didn't die. She looked at him in wonder.

"Asbestos lined," he said. "For spot welding."

The gloves were a murky white and extended halfway up the woman's arms. She thought them the most beautiful gloves in the world. "Did your nephew think this up?" she said.

"No."

"The UN?"

Maître Robichaud laughed. "I do have some good ideas on my own, you know." He said he would be back every night for the rest of the week, and put a business card on the table with a phone number she could reach him at any time. On the back was another number, for a supermarket that delivered.

He left at nine o'clock; it was already quite dark. The Blooms were in their bedroom, making up.

At the end of the week, after they had eaten together every night, Maître Robichaud announced he was in love with the woman and wished to kiss her. She felt the same way about him, but she was terrified: what if her lips had the same effect as her hands? He scoffed at this. She continued to object, so he had her kiss the azalea. Nothing happened. So she put on the asbestos gloves and they kissed. For a moment, she thought she might die herself. (After all, she was twenty-six years old and hadn't kissed anyone since her parents died almost twenty years earlier. Besides, those had been very different kisses!) But the woman wept and sent Maître Robichaud away, saying it was too dangerous. Maître Robichaud offered to put the world's best minds –

his nephew's, the UN's, and his own – on the question: what had happened when she was six years old that could have caused this dramatic change to her hands and her life? When he discovered the answer to that, he was certain he would know how to heal her.

Maître Robichaud vowed not to return till he fulfilled his quest. Meantime, he told her, perhaps she would think about going back to work? She might also visit the Blooms, who continued asking after her. The woman promised to consider it.

Maître Robichaud telephoned every evening to quiz the woman about her childhood. But it turned out the woman didn't want to remember. The more he pushed, the more she saw her life as a flight from memory. All the reading let other people's lives drown out the few experiences she could recall that were actually hers and, later on, the absence of much of life most people took for granted. But Maître Robichaud persisted as if his own life was at stake, and perhaps it was. He grilled her by phone about movies and television (he had some bizarre notion that a Disney movie had inadvertently harnessed in her the power of suggestion). Another night, he asked about foods she had tried – maybe it was some weird kind of allergic reaction, or an autoimmune thing. During yet another conversation, he told her to "close your eyes and think back to that night, your sixth birthday."

"I'm closing my eyes," she said.

"There's the cake," he told her. "Try to see it. Do you see it?"

"Yes. It's beautiful. Chocolate with pink icing roses."

"Who's carrying it?"

"What?"

"Who is bringing it toward you, your mother or your father?"

"What does that matter?"

"I'm just trying to—"

"I'm not sure what you're trying to do. Indulge this morbid fetish of yours? Make me feel like even more of a freak?"

"I'm trying to help you," he said. "Now close your eyes."

"But what if I don't *want* to remember?"

"You are not a freak," he said. "How many candles?"

"It was my sixth birthday," she snapped. "How many would you expect?"

"Some families add an extra one. For good luck."

"Well, weren't we the lucky ones?" she said. "I'm sorry, I just can't do this right now. I've got to go."

Robichaud, surprised by the catch in her voice, said goodbye. "Think about hypnosis, though," he added.

"Good*night*," she said.

Robichaud pursued other avenues, badgering his UN contacts for help, relentlessly. They referred him, eventually, to the World Health Organization, which was no help at all: sorry, they told him, but they only researched medical conditions that affected millions of people.

Of course, being in love with the woman, Maître Robichaud couldn't keep away for long. A week after his vow, he found her enjoying an early fall barbeque at the Blooms'. They were drinking brandy (VSOP) and, after all the red wine she had consumed that evening, the woman was tipsy. Maître Robichaud sat in his dark suit with his dark hair, watching the woman talk and laugh, touching her lips, running her hands through her curls. The asbestos gloves lay on the floor beside her; she was unable to hold a knife or fork, wineglass or brandy snifter while wearing them. He watched her slim hands so intently that he made her self-conscious. Meanwhile, the icicle lights twinkled like fireflies.

When it was time to go, Gary brought out a cutting of the rambling rose bush from the front of his house, the little plant quivering in its crystal vase, to say he would plant it for her in the spring, when its roots were more robust. The woman looked at her hands for a moment, the nails trim and limned with white as though slivers of the moon had taken up residence on the tips of her fingers. Then she told the Blooms how grateful she was.

Before they left, the woman slipped the gloves back on. Still, she felt anxious when Maître Robichaud insisted on taking her arm; she didn't like him to touch her much, aside from the kissing, though of course she really wanted much more. She'd read Bronte and Austen (and, if it must be told, consumed *Cosmopolitan* and Harlequin romances like potato chips, delivered in brown paper by UPS and furtively recycled).

It was chilly as they crossed the lawn, stars trembling in the deepening dark. The woman stumbled and Maître

Robichaud grabbed her waist. Had Maître Robichaud discovered something about her condition, was that why he was here and so, so, so brooding?

"Not really. We should talk inside," he said.

At her door, she shook off a glove and fished the key from her pocket, but in her flustered, somewhat besotted state, dropped it on the porch. Maître Robichaud retrieved it and opened the door, stepping aside to let her in.

"How gallant," she said.

"Put it back on," he said, offering the glove. He closed the door. She did as he asked and was taken by surprise as he stepped forward to kiss her and push her up against the closed door. They kissed and kissed, more than they ever had before. She felt a slippery throb between her legs, beating in a wet rhythm with her heart. Her nipples, even her tongue felt it. "We can't do this," she said, "it's too dangerous."

He drew away and looked into her eyes. "Do you want to return to a life of books, without me, without this?"

Of course she didn't. Who would?

"Then let me tie you to the bed," he said. "That old brass bed of yours, I've been imagining tying you there for days. Trust me," he said, "trust me."

She demurred, but he kissed her again, burning a trail along her jaw and neck, then pinning her arms above her head. He ground his body into hers; if he hadn't been holding her against the oaken door, she would have slipped to the floor, swooned, she would have, she would have, no doubt.

They went up to her bedroom. Maître Robichaud lit a candle he'd brought, casting moody flickers over heaps of books and across the ceiling. She took off her gloves and her clothes, put the gloves back on, and he removed his clothes. A pilaster of Naipul, Rushdie, and Roth toppled to the floor as he pulled the white chenille bedspread and blankets off the bed in one feral movement. He placed a pillow at the head of the bed and she lay down, arms extended. He used the tie he'd been wearing for her left arm and a scarf of hers for her right. She made him swear not to touch her arms below the elbows. He swore.

He backed away from the bed and looked at her, spread-eagled, her breasts like filled goblets, her rose-tipped nipples, the darkness of her mons. "Make sure they're tight enough," she said, pulling against the ties.

"You look…" he said. "Luscious," he said, "yes, luscious," and she moaned.

But then he told her to wait and left the room. The woman was tied up, all she could do was wait, wait and worry, first only a little, then more than that. To take her mind off things (would he come back or had he simply left her there? How ridiculous, she knew his suit was in a puddle on the pink rug beside the bed!), she started thinking about the novel she'd just started reading, *The Hummingbird's Daughter*.

When Maître Robichaud returned minutes later, the azalea in one hand, the olive oil in the other, he realized at once she was doing that distancing thing. "Stop it," he said.

"This is your life, this is our life." She soon forgot about anything else as he ran the azalea over her lips, her cheek, down her neck and collar bone, then lower, to circle her nipples. None of the leaves or petals died.

She saw his erection and wondered what penetration would feel like, if it would hurt. But she wasn't afraid, and she had a brief image of herself as a living crucifix, then she spread her legs in invitation to his hands and tongue and, for once, stopped thinking completely.

Some time later, just after Maître Robichaud helped her turn onto her stomach, her arms still firmly out of reach, he spread her legs again, poured the olive oil into the curve of her back and massaged it across her hips and her buttocks and into the clefts between her legs. As Maître Robichaud finally, achingly, lowered himself onto her, into her, she writhed and called out a passage from Ginsburg at the precise moment that, across the street, the icicle lights glimmering in miniature constellations, in their own king-sized bed, Jake breathed the same line into Gary.

As autumn segued to winter, Maître Robichaud and the woman enjoyed a period of contentment. They had their work, their love affair, their friendship with the Blooms, their hobbies – to her regular reading she added gardening books, and together they planned for the spring, while he gave her an autographed copy of Coltrane's 1962 *Ballads*, worth a small fortune – and they even had family as he introduced her to his nephew, his brother, and his sister-in-law. (As she refused to wear the asbestos gloves in public, the visit passed in a torment of apprehension.) The lovers were happy in even the most mundane occupations – raking leaves, planting crocus bulbs, putting away lawn furniture. But, being only human, theirs was a happiness that could not last. To each and every version of paradise there is a unique serpent spoiler.

The woman gradually became frustrated over Maître Robichaud's relentless effort to understand her deadly hands, while for his part Maître Robichaud chafed at all the time she spent reading and became dissatisfied with the limits her affliction imposed on their love-making. The woman, afraid of touching him in the turnings of intimacy, insisted her hands be tied to the bedposts. Maître Robichaud was startled to discover after a while that he pined for more pedestrian loving contact: the casual hug, the blessing of falling asleep tucked together like spoons, of waking to find himself in her embrace.

By February, the darkest month, the lovers were sniping at one another with regularity. Maître Robichaud wanted to move in, but the woman refused. More than anything, she wished never to hurt him. She was sure if they were together too much, they might grow complacent, careless.

"I'm sick to death of discussing my childhood," she told him, stir-frying a chicken and vegetable dish one evening. "Constantly rehashing my parents' deaths. Besides, who really remembers much from when they were six years old?"

"My nephew does," said Maître Robichaud.

"Oh, for God's sake," said the woman, banging her wooden spoon down on a mess of cookbooks and turning on him. "Your nephew's ten years old!" She wore a white skirt and low-cut white blouse (he liked her all in white, that she knew), with a full skirt cinched tight at the waist (ditto) and black fishnet stockings with four-inch heels (ditto squared).

Maître Robichaud stared for a long moment. Tea lights guttered on a linen spread garnished with four place settings. "I don't suppose you'd like to go upstairs?"

She said, "The Blooms are coming over."

"Yes, of course." He eyed her deliberately. "What about right here?"

"No," she said.

He turned and slung his suit jacket over the back of a chair, loosened his tie, and went to the fridge in search of the wine. "I understand," he said.

"I don't think you do," she said.

He opened and closed a kitchen cupboard. "Where are all the glasses?"

"In the dishwasher, for Christ's sake."

"Your language," he said. "You're breaking one of my cardinal rules."

"I didn't realize you were in professional conflict resolution mode. Anyway, this is still my house," she flung back, "and I'll say whatever I bloody well choose, any way I choose to fucking say it," (She'd been nervous that evening and had started drinking before he arrived.)

Maître Robichaud retrieved the glasses from the dishwasher. He opened the utensil drawer to comment on the mess inside.

"If you don't like it, there's the door, don't let me stop you." She kept her back to him, busy at the stove.

"Don't talk nonsense," he said.

"Anyone ever tell you you're impossible to argue with?"

"I've lived in war zones," he said. "I've stood between people ready to cut each other to pieces. I've stared down the barrel of a gun, of a hundred guns. As problems go, this is nothing much."

"Nothing much…"

"I mean it's hardly insurmountable." The cork popped (he'd found the corkscrew in the rat's nest of a drawer). "Maybe this'll help." He brought her some wine and kissed the side of her neck.

She pulled away.

He sat at the table, leaning over to unlace his shoes.

She stirred the rice, and banged the pot lid down. "I'm pregnant," she said.

He straightened up with alacrity. "You're kidding."

She turned and looked at him. "Why would I joke about this?"

"I'm just… surprised, is all."

"You're surprised," she said.

"Not unpleasantly," he said.

"Oh, well. So long as you're okay with it."

"And you're not?"

"I'm having an abortion," she said.

"But why?"

"It's not enough to have a lover I can't caress, you also expect me be the mother of a child I can never really touch?"

"Let me call the Blooms, put them off a week."

"Screw the Blooms."

"They aren't really my type."

A strangled sound issued from the woman's throat. The doorbell rang. "Send them away," she said.

Maître Robichaud left the kitchen. The woman heard murmuring. She wiped her eyes with a paper towel. Shoes banged sloppily along the hardwood hallway. Then, before she was ready, he was back, leaning against the doorframe. "'Woman trouble,' I told them. I doubt they bought it."

"I'm in trouble all right." She pointed her spoon at his feet. "Your laces are undone."

He looked down, then back at her. "We should talk."

"Don't you have a set of special rules to govern this discussion?" She grabbed her wineglass and gulped down half its contents.

"Should you be drinking in your condition?"

"You think every problem can be solved by negotiation?"

"Pretty much."

"Get out of here," she said. "Please. Just get out."

Maître Robichaud went.

Over the next three days, he phoned her thirty-seven times. She never answered, never returned his calls. He resorted to sending letters, which she returned, marked "undeliverable." She wouldn't come to the door when he rang (he thought using his key might be over-stepping it). The Blooms phoned to tell him her walk remained unshovelled, her newspapers accumulating at the front door. Early on, Gary saw her open a second-storey window and pitch a clutch of long-stemmed red roses into the snow, where they lay like blood spatter from a suicide. "Ah," Robichaud said, clearing his throat, "then she *did* get them."

One afternoon, Jake pounded on the door, a box of groceries against his hip – milk, decaf coffee ground for a French press, Toblerone, peaches, mangoes and strawberries. The woman opened the door. She thanked him, swaying silently for a moment, eyes brown-circled, hair straggly. She wore a pink silk kimono. She said, "Tell him I got rid of it," and shut the door.

Weeks passed. Maître Robichaud shovelled her walk and cancelled her newspaper subscriptions. He kept calling: Did she want him to bring her food, books, magazines, jazz CDs? After another ten of these daily messages, she finally responded, asking him to please bring her some spiced olives, Macadamia nuts, and Miles Davis, mentioning in passing that she hadn't the heart for reading anymore. Maître Robichaud was shocked – reading had consumed at least four hours of her day, even after he'd shown up – but he was relieved she would speak with him again, that she would let him bring her things, even if it was only to the front porch.

Another month passed. The snow was almost history; everywhere the lawns were reduced to muddy brown pulp.

In early April, Maître Robichaud squared his shoulders as he mounted the stairs to the woman's small cottage. He rang the doorbell. After a moment, a window on the second floor scraped open.

"Who's there?" she called.

He backed down the stairs so they could see each other.

"Go away," she said.

"I'm coming in," he said, holding up his key. The door swung inward and he followed it, calling, "Where are you?"

"You know perfectly well where I am," said the woman, coming down the stairs.

Maître Robichaud said, "I've had just about enough of this."

The woman's laugh reverberated as she came down the staircase. "I bet you practised that line all the way over here."

He flushed.

Her pink silk kimono hung open over a white flannel nightdress that came to her knees. She was barefoot and free of makeup but her hair looked clean enough. There was the distinct smell of lemon in the air.

"I'm waxing the floors," she said. "I found this big old electric floor polisher in the basement, with sheepskin pads for buffing. It's surprisingly relaxing," she said.

"Really," he said.

"You think I'm crazy."

"Now why would I think that? Just because you've holed yourself up here for four months, ignoring my phone calls and letters—"

"I answered your phone calls."

"After three months of nothing," he said.

She slumped suddenly on the stairs. "I'm sorry," she murmured. "I get light-headed sometimes."

"Are you eating enough?"

"No worries on that score. Maybe I have low blood pressure every now and again."

"Not enough fresh air," he said. "Not enough sunlight, or vitamin D."

"It's winter," she said. "No one gets enough sunlight or vitamin D."

"It's spring," he corrected. "Can't we stop this sniping and have the conversation we should have had four months ago? Please?"

She looked at him, shrugged and sighed, then took hold of the banister. She stood up. She swayed. "Oh," she said. "I'm afraid I'm going to—"

He lunged forward as she plummeted down past the last four stairs. He didn't quite catch her, but he did manage to break her fall. For a moment, they lay tangled on the polished floor, Maître Robichaud on his back, the woman heaped on top of him.

She pushed herself up, one hand on his chest and the other on the floor. "Oh, my God," she cried, snatching her hand away. "I've touched you. I knew this would happen, I knew it!"

He lifted his head off the floor and, after a couple of beats, said, "No, I'm okay. I didn't feel anything."

"Really?" She sat up cross-legged beside him, putting a hand to her forehead to smooth her hair.

"Let me help you," he said, standing up. He held out a hand. She looked at it leerily, so he said, "Shall I hoist you up under your arms, then?"

She nodded, and he went behind her to lift her upright. She held her hands before her as though just having scrubbed for the operating room. Robichaud leaned in and nuzzled her neck. He inhaled deeply (lemon floor wax, pleasant nonetheless). He slipped his arms around her middle and hoisted her upright.

"I really must sit," she said, making for the living room.

Maître Robichaud stood where she left him as though rooted to the spot.

After a moment, the woman asked if he was coming. He walked slowly and sat across from her (pushing a stash of Agatha Christies to the floor). He stared off into the middle distance.

"What?" she said.

"You didn't… get rid of it," he said finally.

"No," she said. "It's started to kick. You can feel it if you like." She used both her hands to pull the flannel taut over her abdomen.

Maître Robichaud stared his black-eyed stare.

"I think it's a girl," she said. Her eyes sparked, enigmatic galaxies.

He went over to sit beside her, tossing aside some issues of the now-defunct *Gourmet* and a novel by Ha Jin. She picked up his hand and placed it on the curve of her. "Feel that?"

He nodded. "Is it because you're pregnant?"

"What? My hands?"

Again he nodded. The baby kicked vigorously. (Even without sunlight, even without vitamin D!)

"Possibly, but I really hate the thought that that's the explanation."

Robichaud raised his eyebrows but said nothing.

"Hardly an acceptable solution, for a feminist. I prefer to think it's the reading. Or rather, the not-reading. After we quarrelled, I was so sick at heart about everything, I couldn't read anything at all," she explained. "I slept, mostly. And a month or so after I gave up reading, there was this weird tingling in my hands." She experimented with the azalea and deduced that reading more than two hours per day re-established her hands' deadly capacity. Otherwise, she was fine. She began thinking about keeping the baby.

"And then, over the course of a few days and nights, I saw what had happened. In daydreams, in nightmares…"

"Your sixth birthday?"

"Exactly." She'd only had dribs and drabs of it, she said – *Matilda*, the tented sheets. In fact, she'd pushed even traces of these memories away as much as she could. For years.

Maître Robichaud slipped his hand into hers.

"No," the woman said. "Let me get this out." She walked over to the living room window, pushed the sheers aside and stood there with her back to him. "That night, the night of my sixth birthday, we had my favourite dinner – fish and chips. And radishes."

"Radishes?"

"Don't get distracted. I happen to have liked radishes," she said. "Then the cake, shiny chocolate icing with pink roses. My mother made it all herself and carried it into the darkened dining room. Her face glowing, almost supernatural. It was the candles, of course. It was dark and she put the cake down before me and both of them sang to me, bathed in candlelight. That's the way I want to remember them. Remember me."

After a moment, Robichaud couldn't wait anymore. "And?"

"Did I ever tell you they tried for nearly ten years to get pregnant? I found my mother's diary. She kept one from the time she was a young woman." This time Robichaud just waited.

The woman pulled her robe round her, belting and folding her arms beneath her breasts. From where he sat, it looked as though she was hugging herself.

"So. The cake, the books. And they put me to bed."

He waited.

"After they kissed me goodnight, I pulled a large camping flashlight up from under my bed and got the new books down from my bookshelf. When they found me some time later, they said I had to stop reading. I said no way, it was my birthday. My mother said that didn't matter, it was much too late already, it was nearly midnight and it was a school night..." She sighed. "And I started to shout. I had never felt so angry before. Like my chest had filled with fire. And I shrieked and carried on like a little hellion, I'm afraid. My dad came running in – they were both in their pyjamas – and they tried to calm me down… but it was the first time I'd ever read books completely on my own and I didn't *want* to stop, I *would not* stop, you see. And this white heat, this lava, gushed through me and I shrieked as they tried to take the books away. They told me that if I behaved myself, I'd get the books back the next day, but if I didn't, I would never get them back." The woman took a deep breath and sighed. "I was kicking and scratching, spitting like a wet cat. It took both of them to pry the books away from me. And then I told them that I hated them. And they laughed. They laughed!

"I told them that I hated them so much, I wished they were dead! And then I jumped at them and suddenly… they were."

Maître Robichaud came and put his arm around her at the window. "My dear," he said. He kissed her hair. He became aware of the clock ticking away on the mantle.

"And I just knew I had to keep this baby. I got down on my knees and shouted 'Glory, hallelujah, and praise the Lord!'"

"Did you really?"

"Don't be an idiot," she said. "Are you happy about it?"

"The baby?"

"Yes, of course, the baby."

Robichaud all at once became aware of the scene unfolding before their bay window: Gary Bloom puttering out front as Jake came onto the porch and they had a few emphatic exchanges. Gary lifting the binoculars from around his neck and passing them up to Jake. Jake waggling the binoculars in a raised hand, firing off a final verbal salvo before re-entering the house. Gary shook his head and looked over at the woman's cottage.

Maître Robichaud placed his palm against the glass. "Get dressed," he said. "Let's go tell the Blooms that they're going to be uncles."

His arms opened wide in front of him, palms upward, Gary shrugged. And then he waved back.

END

ACADEMIC FREEDOM

Marie's breath billowed through the November rain as she mounted the steps, grocery bags spilling from her arms. She'd forgotten the reusable bags again and at the check-out had asked for paper, the environmentally responsible choice. Now the bags were soggy and so was she. When she'd set off an hour earlier, Nigel assured her he'd be there to help, but, as the doorbell echoed through their Montreal cottage, there was no sign of him. Marie swore *sotto voce*, trying to finagle her house key into a lock she could not see. She hated it when Nigel was unreliable, her irritation leavened with the fear he was morphing into a forgetful old git.

Finally, blind fumbling found its mark. Keys jangled, tumblers fell, the door swung inward. Marie, shivering, spent the next ten minutes unloading the car. After that she phoned Nigel's cell. Lately he seemed even more distracted than usual, but Marie put it down to the latest crop of "tenure-seeking pipsqueaks" – Nigel's words – hot on his neck, making him feel his age. The dean had suggested early retirement several times in recent years, each time a little more emphatically. After the last of these little chats, Nigel, with a tight smile, told Marie, "There's no way I'm leaving before that bitch does." But Marie wanted Nigel to retire, convinced it was time they relaxed a bit and did some travelling. She wanted to see the rain forests, to cruise the Panama Canal.

No answer. Marie shuddered, pushing a hand through her sodden, mousy hair. Nigel had been after her to colour it; so far, she had refused. Replacing the receiver, Marie realized she'd heard the distinctive ring of Nigel's cell – Beethoven's Fifth – from somewhere in the house. This really steamed her: what was the point of the phone if he left it at home? Of course, Nigel resented it, called it a "second umbilicus."

Marie decided what she needed was a hot shower and a change of clothes. She marched up the stairs and, on her way to the bathroom, passed Nigel's study and noticed his chair overturned. She entered the room and discovered Nigel sprawled face down on the carpet in the study, unconscious, his breathing stentorian. At least he *was* breathing, she thought, moving to turn him over. Then she thought better of it and grabbed at the phone. Waiting for the emergency crew, she sat on the floor stroking his cheek.

The ambulance appeared within minutes, lights flashing, siren off, the young attendants in navy uniforms accessorized with vibrant blue plastic gloves. One of the medics mounted the stairs as Marie followed, relaying the little she knew. He made straight for the patient, narrating his findings to a radio clipped to his shoulder. Marie stood silent in the doorway, clenching and unclenching her hands.

"Bon," said the attendant – he looked so young, surely too young to know anything? – "he's unconscious, but his pulse is strong. Any medical problems? Diabetes, high blood pressure?"

"No, nothing like that," Marie answered, frowning. Nigel didn't tell her everything. He was a great believer in the virtue of having a private life. Marie respected that; there were probably things about him she was better off not knowing.

"We'll take him to emergency," the young man told Marie. "Today it's the General, okay?"

Marie nodded.

The two attendants struggled to get the stretcher up the stairs, collapsed it onto the floor, and turned Nigel over, preparatory to settling him on it. That's when Marie noticed Nigel's pants were undone, his penis hanging out, a conspicuous white crudescence smeared across his lap of brown corduroy.

"*Colisse, qu'est-ce qui s'est passé?*" one of the attendants exclaimed, looking up at her. Marie recoiled, feeling cold, then hot.

"What happened?" the other one repeated.

"Nothing," she said. Then, hearing how lame that sounded, added, "I have absolutely no idea."

In short order, Nigel was wrapped in a red blanket and secured to the stretcher, an oxygen mask obscuring the pale moon of his face. Trembling a little, shock added now to the chill, Marie trailed them down the stairs and outside. The circling red lights cast an eerie glow; darkness was falling.

The medic turned to her after closing the ambulance doors, an unusual expression on his face. Was it… pity?

"You're welcome to come with us."

How would she feel, stuck next to these strangers for the fifteen-minute drive? Her thinking was all muddled; Marie knew she was obsessing over small details to avoid surrender to the larger ones. "No," she said, abandoning the shower but determined at least to find some dry clothing. "I'll drive myself over momentarily. The General, right?"

"He's quite stable, Madame. Everything will be okay."

She found the comment formulaic and hard to believe.

Marie made her way up the stairs as though swimming upstream, her head throbbing with questions. From the study doorway, Marie stared at a mark on the navy rug. She fetched a dampened cloth and rubbed at the stain, then sat back on her knees, lamenting their stiffness. Her attention was attracted by "3D pipes," the screensaver filling the monitor. She righted the chair and sat down with a sigh. She should just turn it off, shouldn't she? Let it remain a surface thing.

Not bloody likely, she decided after a moment. She jiggled the mouse. The screen resolved into a chat room called "Underage fun."

> Dean: let me b the 1st to slip a finger in ur tight young cunt.

(From the colour of the text, Marie could tell it was Nigel who had responded.)

Samantha-I-am: only 1?

Marie's posture became more and more extreme as she scrolled through the "conversation." Elbows on desk, she leaned her head in her hands for a moment, then sighed and sat up straight again. She copied and pasted the entire chat into a Word file. While it printed, she gazed out the window into the darkening night.

By the time she arrived at the hospital, Nigel had had blood work, and Marie was told he was being admitted to neurology; an MRI had been scheduled.

"Probable TIA," the resident told her, explaining this was shortspeak for transient ischemic attack. Nigel's brain had been deprived of oxygen, causing him to black out. Rare in someone under seventy but not unheard of, serious but not life-threatening. It was often related to calcification of the blood network supplying the brain. Nigel's risk of stroke would be assessed. "He's resting comfortably, probably come out of it within twelve hours or so. You should go home, get some rest yourself. We'll call you if anything changes. I suppose you'd like to see him?"

After a moment Marie said, "No, I don't believe I would."

On leaving the hospital, Marie drove aimlessly for a while. She came to on Remembrance Road. The car, as though on autopilot, had brought her to the belvedere overlooking

Montreal's East End. She got out of the car. She was glad the rain had let up. She gazed out over her city, standing next to a collection of cherubic Spanish-speakers, the darkness lit stroboscopically as they snapped smiling photos of one another. The city shimmered, a carpet of multi-coloured light and energy, dissipating. Montreal drove her crazy sometimes, with its loopy self-appointed vigilantes on their mission to guard the city's French face, but she knew after a lifetime here, she would never leave. She felt the same way about Nigel. Maybe this episode was a harbinger of dementia. Thoughts of Alzheimer's were ubiquitous among people her age. Marie had been reading up on it: uncharacteristic conduct could be a sign.

When she again felt the cold, she drove down from the mountain toward home, suddenly deciding on a detour to her neighbourhood police station. She told the young woman at the desk she wished to report a pedophile. Marie declined to take a seat. She paced until she was brought to a small office occupied, she saw with relief, by a man in his early sixties, the same age as Nigel. The man rose from behind the desk.

"Detective Brisebois," he said, holding out his hand.

"Marie Caran," she said, taking it. "I hope you're as unflappable as you look."

"Please," he indicated a chair, "what can I do for you?"

"A pedophile," she said, sitting down, all at once rather faint. She had missed dinner. And suddenly, it was hard even to swallow. "I must report a pedophile. Could I have some water," she croaked, turning to the constable who had escorted her, "please?"

Bottled water was duly fetched. Marie looked at it glumly. "Tap water would have been sufficient," she said.

"*Comment?*" said the detective.

"Never mind," said Marie. She drank half the bottle, wiping her mouth with the back of her hand.

"A pedophile?" the detective prompted.

Marie dug through her purse and pulled out the chatscript. For a moment was loath to hand it over. "It's my husband," she said.

"Are you saying, Madame, that your husband's a pedophile?"

"No." She gave the detective the papers. "But he's involved with one."

While the detective glanced through the document, Marie thought about Nigel's career at the university, the awards and accolades, the promise everyone had seen in him, herself included. Once those nature-nurture arguments had electrified them both; anything had seemed possible. But that was long ago. There was no longer any scope for big men, big ideas. Now biology was molecular, choked with minutiae, or so Nigel said. Nanotechnology, he'd scoff, no longer really engaged. But he was a proud man and a competitive one, maybe too stubborn to pack it in. Was there really something wrong with his brain, something that made sense of all this?

"Mrs. Caran, perhaps you can explain this to me," said the detective. "This is a conversation between a fourteen-year-old girl and an older man, right? Are you telling me this man is your husband?"

"Not exactly," Marie answered. "Actually, my husband is the fourteen-year-old girl."

"*Pardon?*"

"My husband. I think he was playing the role of a fourteen-year-old girl. The person he was talking to thought he was a child. *That* person is the pedophile."

The detective re-read the transcript. He passed a hand over his forehead, followed through by smoothing his hair, what was left of it. He sighed. "Mme. Caran, it's been a long day. Just tell me what you think happened. Please."

Marie didn't like the way this was phrased, but resolved to do her best.

Next morning, Nigel was sitting up in bed, picking at his hospital breakfast as Marie arrived. His face brightened when he saw her. "Marie, darling," he said heartily. "I've been anxious to see you. What on earth happened last night? I must have given you quite a turn." He puckered up, expectantly.

"I won't kiss you, Nigel," she said, patting his shoulder. "I've caught a chill, I may be coming down with something. How are you feeling?" Marie pulled a chair up beside the bed and sat down, putting her purse on her lap.

He unpuckered. "Fine, absolutely first class. Slept like a log." He peered at her. "You're looking a little peaky though, my dear."

"Well," she said, "I haven't had the best night."

"Oh, darling, I am *so* sorry for frightening you like that."

Marie looked at him sharply. "Don't you remember anything?"

"No, not really. Nothing after your going… where was it?"

"Grocery shopping, remember?"

"And then?"

"That's what I want to ask you."

The resident walked in then and offered them a brief report. Nigel would be released that afternoon. He needed a follow-up appointment with a neurologist.

"So he's not in any danger? It's not a sign of something more serious?" Marie asked. The doctor blathered several mouthfuls of reassurance and breezed back out the door.

"Good news that, isn't it, my dear?"

"Nigel," said Marie with intensity, "don't you remember," her voice dropped, "*Samantha*?"

"No," he answered, busy again with his breakfast. "Should I?" He made a face. "Heavens, Marie, these eggs are dreadful. Nothing like yours." He poked them with the fork, looking dubious. "If they are eggs."

"*Nigel*," said Marie.

He looked up at her. "You needn't shout, my dear. I'm right here, perfectly attentive, all bright-eyed and bushy-tailed."

Bushy-tailed! Marie thought she might have a stroke herself. "Nigel, you don't remember anything about Samantha?"

"Samantha," he said, looking thoughtful. "Don't think I do, no. Unless you mean that old Dr. Seuss character? 'That Sam-I-am, that Sam-I-am, I do not like that Sam-I-am.'"

"Nigel, be serious."

"'Do you like green eggs and ham?' That's it, *that's* how dreadful this breakfast is. 'Not in a car, not in a box, not in the rain.'" He chanted rhythmically, fork slicing the air like a conductor's baton. "How does that go again?"

"For God's sake, Nigel," Marie fumed, "under the circumstances, I'd hardly be quoting children's books." She pulled the dog-eared transcript from her purse, handing it to him.

"You know I can't read anything without my glasses," Nigel said with mild reproach. "D'you think you could read it to me?"

"No," Marie answered, "I can't."

Nigel looked mystified.

"Nigel, have you ever used the Internet for—" she paused, leaning toward him – "*sex*?"

Nigel's fork clattered to the tray. "Marie, my dear," he said. "I know this must be very stressful for you, but have you lost your mind?"

Heaven help me, Marie thought, if whatever he's got doesn't do it, I'll kill him myself.

Ten days passed as Nigel's memory slowly returned. It was an experiment, he explained, something he'd wanted to try ever since watching a segment about cybersex on *Sixty Minutes*. But Marie pressed her advantage, insisting the blackout had been "a wake-up call."

"More like an unconsciousness call," Nigel pointed out. They both laughed – though to Marie, this felt like whistling through a graveyard. Nigel finally agreed that perhaps this was a good time to consider retiring. Over the next few days they thrashed things through, reaching another of those reasonable accommodations that permitted long-term marriages to endure.

Several weeks later, Friday late-afternoon, Detective Brisebois paid a visit to the Carans' household. "You're looking exceptionally well, Madame," he said, stamping his boots free of snow. Marie placed his overcoat on a wooden coat rack and escorted him to the living room. "Nigel," she called, "it's the detective."

Brisebois stared at Marie for a moment. "Have you done something to your hair?"

"Yes, actually. I've coloured it. What do you think?" She ran a hand through newly auburned curls, looking like the cat that got the cream.

"*Très chic*, I would say."

"I couldn't agree more. She looks fantastic, decades younger," Nigel chimed in, ushering the detective to the red velvet settee and settling in beside him.

Brisebois picked up a brochure from among several on the coffee table. "Going somewhere?"

"Always the detective," Marie said with a smile as she sat across from them. "Nigel's retiring and we're going to travel. We may take a cruise, visit Costa Rica, the rainforest. I've always been interested in things ecological."

"Congratulations," Brisebois said. "I'm sure you'll both enjoy that." He turned to face Nigel. "I just came by to tell you the name of the other party involved in your little charade. I think you'll find this amusing." He leaned over to whisper in Nigel's ear.

"Good lord," Nigel burst out, "*the Dean*?! I wondered why she was leaving so precipitately."

"She said she'd been engaged in 'preforensic sociological research on pedophiles,'" Brisebois said with a shake of his head.

Nigel snorted. "What rubbish! She's a world authority on nematode homeoboxes."

Brisebois looked perplexed. "On what?"

"The nematode. A type of worm, Detective. The Dean's an expert on body pattern genes in worms. Light-years away from 'preforensic sociological research,' whatever that is."

The detective smiled, a trifle sadly, Marie thought. "A worm expert, eh? That's perfect, *esti*." He sighed. "I'm getting too old for this job. I've never found myself so continually disappointed by human nature." He fingered another brochure. "The Galapagos, eh? There's a trip I've always dreamt of, ever since Watson and Crick won the Nobel when I was a boy."

"Watson, Crick, and Maurice Wilkins, Detective," Nigel chimed in.

"Wasn't there someone the committee overlooked, some woman, as I recall?" said Marie.

"Quite right, Marie darling. Rosamund Franklin, if memory serves. Tragedy really, being passed over like that," Nigel added.

"It's a man's world, isn't it, Detective? Perhaps a drink would restore your faith in humankind."

Brisebois smiled. "Thank you, Madame. That just might do the trick."

Brisebois assented to scotch and Marie rose to busy herself with a crystal cross-and-olive patterned decanter and some matching glasses in the dining room. "Ice, Detective, or water?" She had to raise her voice a bit to overcome the distance between them.

"Water, please."

"We're here for a good time, not a long time, Detective," she called to him, amid companionable clinking. "And as there was no actual child involved, no harm done." She walked back, placed a silver tray on the coffee table and handed round the tumblers of amber liquid.

"Of course, you are right, Madame. Amazing though, how society has changed. A middle-aged woman impersonating a lecherous old man, and an older—"

"Middle-aged," Nigel all-but-shouted.

"*Bien, un homme d'un certain age,* then, acting the part of a fourteen-year-old girl. And somehow, across the miracle of cyberspace, they find their next-door neighbours to engage in dirty talk. What are the chances of that?"

"Infinitesimal, I should think," Nigel said. "But when you consider how unlikely it is life's arisen on Earth at all, anything seems possible."

The detective *tsked*, shaking his head again. He raised his glass to the Carans and took a good long pull.

"So long as there was no real crime," Marie said, sitting at the edge of her chair.

"Not this time," the detective allowed. He put his glass down on the Galapagos brochure. "Still, it wasted the better part of a day of technician time, not to mention mine. With all the problems in the world, you'd think these professors would have more important things to do."

"Oh yes," Nigel replied, smacking his lips, "you would, wouldn't you?"

CARBON-DATED, GOLD-PLATED

In the furnace room, Jane struggled to get past a lean-to of sporting equipment from the year dot – tent poles, cross-country skis, hockey sticks, tennis racquets, and several pairs of traditional wood-and-rawhide snowshoes. It was an awkward manoeuvre that ended in a premature cacophony as an elbowed toboggan dove to the cement floor. Jane froze. Sure enough, within seconds, Bill's voice wafted from the doorway at the top of the stairs.

"Jane? Sure you don't need some help down there?"

Shit no, she thought, but what she said was, "No, dear. Just having a final look round."

"I'll be in the garage if you need me."

"Uh-huh," Jane said, trying to right the tangle. *Liar, faker, phoney,* went the voice in her head.

Jane, who had always nursed the sneaking suspicion junk grew to fit the space available, was still dismayed at the stockpile they had accumulated over thirty-some-odd years – vintage computers, a mouldering canvas tent, boxes of outgrown clothes and toys with labels like "summer '78," and behind that, their cast-off furniture. Why hadn't they gotten rid of things as they'd outgrown them? She sighed. She knew it had to do with the era she'd grown up in.

Her hair tucked in a Wedgwood blue bandana, Jane wore what Bill called "the uniform": her Liz Claiborne denim skirt, so well-used it was almost white, and her oldest, most comfortable cashmere sweater in a pleasing shade of coral. Slipping it over her head, she remembered Bill had always liked her in that colour. These days, though, he hardly looked at her. Maybe she should already be accustomed to it, this damping down of Eros, but desire still bothered her sometimes, throbbing like a toothache. She did her best to suppress the feeling. It was a way of dealing with the world she had perfected.

Bill pottered about the garage, muttering as he sorted through his golf clubs and power tools. Choosing among them was an impossible task. He knew he'd end up sacrificing one or two of them, but purely for the sake of form. He turned, stubbed a toe on a sledge hammer, and swore out loud.

Jane shook her head at the imprecation. She couldn't hear exactly what he'd said but she knew him well enough to fill in the blank. God, but he was becoming positively curmudgeonly. Just that morning, he'd come back inside after clearing the snow from the car, spluttering expletives. "Damn winter and damn those blue-collar workers! They pass by so fast in their little sidewalk ploughs, all they do is scrape the ice bare. So at thirty-five dollars an hour, all they do is make the sidewalks even more dangerous. I fell on my bloody ass once already this morning."

"Bill," she'd chided, "your blood pressure."

"My blood pressure? It's the assholic work ethic around here gives me high blood pressure." He shook his head in disgust. "How we made it through all these winters without breaking our necks… and now they're going on strike because the arbitrator's ruled against a four-day workweek. Doesn't anybody understand what binding arbitration is anymore? Or the value of a dollar? Bloody fools." Off he'd gone, still grumbling.

Before he had retired, Jane could hardly remember hearing Bill swear. Now he was in danger of being typecast, a grumpy old man. And just what would that make her? *An old fraud*, the voice chimed in helpfully. She ignored that, too.

Jane cleared through the soon-to-be-cast-offs without raising further alarm. She made it to her objective, that desk she'd bought for college, nearly forty years ago. It had served their sons in turn until each had demanded something better. Battered but serviceable, though not the sort of piece anyone would call an antique. She ran her hand along the grimy surface. More like the kind of furniture you might find in an old motel on a secondary road near a town that had known better days.

She unlocked the desk drawer and pulled out a fruitwood box with mother-of-pearl inlay that once belonged to her grandmother. Inside lay a musty pile of papers. On the top was a photo of Bill, taken not long after they'd met. He looked out at her across the years, lips full, forehead unmarked, his skin taut against jawline and cheekbones. She ran her fingers over him, a plucking in her chest, then put the photo down.

Next came a sheet of paper, unlined, folded in eighths. A typewritten poem (God, how long had it been since she had seen anything typewritten? How long since she had typed anything herself?). It was dated April 2, 1966, addressed to her, about her. The initials MF at the bottom, the title "Time Out" at the top. The paper had yellowed; it *was* more than forty years old, after all.

Jane smiled as she read it, a poem about the night she and MF sat in a diner hour after hour, watching people drift in and out, drinking coffee and "enjoying each other's Company," MF had written. She found it endearing, this particular capitalization. Why not "cach Other's company?"

We were there so long
we became the normal ones,
the others all
tied
to their boring daily routines.
The more they move,
the tighter the binding
We did as we liked
and enjoyed it.
Our epitaph—
we enjoyed it.

Had she really been a person who inspired others to commit poetry?

She remembered meeting MF again, many years later. A formal event, some fundraiser or other. Bill had been a minor celebrity then, involved in local politics, owned a tuxedo. MF had been there too, wife in tow.

Jane conjured a vision of herself in a sinuous black dress, the one that had shown her neck and shoulders to advantage. Her auburn hair had been coiled in a loose chignon. Closing her eyes a moment, she could remember the feel of Bill's fingers tracing currents across her skin.

But MF's wife hadn't been happy, Jane recalled. She'd looked daggers at me. And he had been bald as an egg! Jane tried to remember if MF had shaved his head, the way some men do, but memory failed her – she couldn't dredge up that much detail. All she felt sure of was that he had become a lawyer, a tax lawyer. A short, bald, tax lawyer. But his eyes, the look in his eyes… that had burned her.

She folded the poem back along its creases, and placed it on the desktop with a pat, the poem not taken, then turned back to excavate another layer of her carbon-dated past.

The letter. She'd just arrived in Boston for her first term, a woman who imagined herself immune to "the problem that has no name." She felt shaky reading it. That was probably how she'd felt the first time, too, she thought.

Montreal
September 23, 1966

Dearest Jane,

I have done my best to forget you. Your affair, though brief, wounded me deeply. Only your amazing honesty managed to redeem us both. You must have known how close I was to proposing.

But I still can't get you out of my thoughts, Jane. You're the first one, the only one, for me. I pray you feel the same. I know it may take time but I want you to know that I will wait, Darling. For as long as it takes.

Please let me make it up to you, Jane. We can do it. We can start over, and live a life without secrets, without regrets…

Oh, now that's really rich, said the voice. Jane shook it off.

The letter had arrived at the lowest point of her life, just as she'd realized that nothing was as she had thought it would be – not her courses, not her roommate, certainly not her feelings. And not long after that, Jane had another epiphany, the anguished realization every young woman dreaded most in those days.

Bill wrote weekly after that, wonderfully stilted missives brimming with devotion. But she'd put off seeing him for a whole year, long enough to clear away any drawn-out details… Jane pushed the thoughts away. *Still running,* said the voice in her head. She ignored it.

Finally, defeated, dispirited, her feminist bravado beaten, Jane had consented to Bill's visit, to letting him woo her back to the comforts of home where he promised her what she had come to crave: a placid, uncomplicated life.

Jane folded the letter and put it away. She retrieved a manila envelope that shielded some quality paper, a page that with one caress announced its high rag count. Jane could hardly bear to look at the smudged whorls and calligraphy of it, even after all this time. Random phrases accosted her – her name, "the Commonwealth of Massachusetts" and "Father Unknown." There was a sheaf of other papers too, her only tangible links. Why she had kept them all this time was a mystery, an inscrutability as deep as all her other failures.

She looked away for a moment, visualizing the baby. Or *a* baby, at any rate – tiny balled fists, a frizz of black hair, rosy skin soft as pussy willows. She heard again the echo of her daughter's first cries.

Another of those lies you insist on, the voice jeered.

The truth was she'd been out of it, gassed unconscious, while giving birth. That's how it had been, back then. Now it was different, everything was. Now no one cared if you were married or not. Now everyone and his brother was invited to the delivery, the way her daughters-in-law had invited them. Now Jane was left to wonder why she didn't have even one photograph of the girl, just these meagre scraps that bore witness to the true story of her life.

"JANE!" Bill bellowed.

Jane jumped. "Yes?" she croaked.

"Haven't you finished yet? We're going to be late for Lisa."

"One more minute and I'm all done," Jane called back. Her heart pounded.

"You know how I hate—" Bill started.

"Yes, yes, I know," said Jane. No matter how trivial the engagement, Jane knew, punctuality was Bill's badge of honour.

"We shouldn't keep Lisa waiting," Bill said.

Bill liked to say they had hot- and cold-running real estate agents working on their behalf. Down in Costa Rica, the "hot" agent was searching out the best location and price in condos while, up here, Lisa fielded bids on their home in Montreal West, an eccentric pile filled with touches Martha Stewart had taught a generation of status-seekers to covet: oak floorboards and woodwork, crystal doorknobs, ceiling mouldings that made Jane think of disciplined meringue. But since their boys had left – goodness, she hated to think how long ago now – the house really was much too large for them.

Yes, Lisa was the cold one, in more ways than one. A thoroughly modern young woman. Unattached, independent. Jane had asked if she ever thought about having children. Lisa had laughed and said, "To tell you the truth, my Miata's much less trouble." Jane had to admit, the electric blue car *was* a dazzler, but sometimes she wondered if Lisa had a cash register where her heart should be.

Jane returned everything to the inlaid box. She'd sneak back here later. The lock gave a guilty click as she turned the key.

I will tell Bill, she told herself, for the hundredth, the millionth, time. *Yeah right*, went the numbing commentary. Jane ignored it. Maybe they could still find her, her first-born, her cipher. Maybe she could explain it all. Maybe it wasn't too late.

But outside, in the rush to the car, Jane missed her footing and felt herself in slow-motion freefall. She made a three-point landing on the ice-rimed pavement, knee, hip, skull. She felt the jarring as an earthquake, heard the crack of her own bone.

Bill shouted, "By Christ!"

Pain exploded in her, like fireworks.

Six weeks later, Jane hobbled from the hospital with a cast up to her thigh. Still, after having been in traction for so long, she counted it a blessing just to be upright again, moving under her own steam. Instead of a clean, crosswise break, her femur had shattered down its length. "A very bad thing," the doctors had opined. They were forever mumbling together, nattering at her when all she wanted was to be left alone. They installed a series of metal pins and rods and then, after monitoring her scans, unhappy with the conjured images, they re-opened the incisions, relocating the hardware just days later. "Complicated," pronounced her cabal of doctors, her coven of surgeons. It could have been a diagnosis of her entire life. As a result, she had been out of it, dopey with morphine, for over a month.

Her only consolation was that the morphine, at its height, silenced her constant critic.

Jane grew sick of hospitals, bedpans, nausea, waking in the middle of the night. She grew tired of being exhausted. She tried to tell Bill about the baby on one of those nightmare nights of IV, stitches, and pulsating pain that reminded her of childbirth. Bill hadn't understood. Or had he simply chosen not to? Jane wasn't sure. She remembered him insisting she remain quiet, telling her to save her strength.

"It was an accident," Jane tried to say. *Phony*, her gremlin hissed as the morphine wore off.

"We can talk later," Bill said. "Don't worry. I'll take care of everything."

Home again, Jane lounged on a flowery chintz sofa in the sunroom on the back of the house. Potted geraniums burst with pink blooms, filling the air with their peppery pungency.

They had put off selling the house. No one could predict when Jane would be better, Jane least of all.

Her leg was propped on a hassock, still swollen, the engorged tissues pressing against the nerves, cutting off all feeling. The doctors told her it would come back as she healed. Hopefully. She bent forward to touch the cast. She wanted to penetrate the plaster casing, to feel her leg again.

Jane found herself with too much time to think. She kept wondering whether her leg wasn't the only part of her that was numb. She'd had a pleasant life. She'd tried to protect herself, but maybe she'd gone too far. Maybe she'd been sleep-walking through life, anesthetized, instead.

Jane leaned back, closing her eyes in the languorous warmth. She imagined a beach in Costa Rica, did her best to place herself there, moving freely again. Unencumbered.

Bill and Jane moved slowly up the front walk, her arm on his, the sunlight incandescent, the heady scent of lilacs everywhere.

"Bill," Jane said, "I have to tell you something." Jane teetered slightly, a little unsteady with the cane. But at least the cast was gone; they were just coming home from having had it removed. Though Jane now wore a brace and needed months of physio, the cabal was confident she would regain "the full range of motion." Listening to their prattle, Jane understood what it was she really longed for: the full range of emotion.

"Yes, dear," Bill answered mechanically. "You okay on the stairs?"

"I don't know." Jane gripped the banister, Bill solid beside her; she was glad he was there. She wondered if she had taken him too much for granted.

They made their way inside, the contrasting darkness of the vestibule so great, Jane was momentarily blind. When her vision cleared, the first thing she saw was the doorway to the basement. "Bill," Jane said, "would you help me downstairs?"

"Jane, darling, is that wise? We should sit for a while. I can make tea. We've been at the hospital for hours, you must be worn out and—"

"Bill," Jane interrupted, trying to inject some steel in her voice and marking instead its shocking quaver, "I want to go downstairs. Now."

"To tell the truth, Jane, I don't think you're up to it. The doctor said you should take it easy for a while, your balance is off. And besides, what do you want to go down there for? There's nothing left."

Jane stopped dead, and slowly turned her head to look up at her husband. "What did you say?"

"I called the Sally Ann, they emptied out the basement while you were in the hospital. A couple of months ago, now," Bill told her. "They cleared it all out, just like we'd planned."

What now, Bill thought, what in God's name had he done wrong now? "Come sit down, Jane. You must be worn out," he said.

Jane stood for a long moment. *Idiot*, the voice shrieked, *you left it too long.* "Shut up," Jane cried.

"Jane? Darling? What the devil's going on?"

"Not you," she said to Bill. Her mouth was dry as ashes.

She swayed. Bill grabbed hold of her upper arm, a little too tightly. He was bruising her, but Jane was glad of it, glad to feel something, anything beyond the pounding of her heart, that dreadful clench of muscle threatening to burst through her chest.

Lost, all of it, everything she had.

"You're right," she whispered. "We should sit down. I'm… absolutely worn out."

Jane trembled as they made their silent way to the sunroom. She collapsed in a chair with a groan.

What the hell, Bill thought. Jane was aging, shrinking, deflating right in front of him like a spent balloon. They had taken him aside at the hospital, they had warned him of this. He could still hear them, the doctor's words, cut into his memory: "At her age, it might be a long recovery."

PIE

Some folks say your hands can tell the story of your life. Well, my hands cain't talk, but they've made so many pies, I bet they could do it themselves if you cut 'em off and gave 'em the right ingredients, I sure do.

'Course, I ain't made pie in going on forty years now. But for me, pie's like ridin' a bike: it's something I'll never forget.

It's the crust ever'one frets on. You got to measure out two cups of flour and a teaspoon salt. Exactly. Eamon liked to tease me about this. He'd say, "Been making pie long?"

And I'd go, "My whole life entire."

And he'd say, "And you still measuring?"

There's things I did by feel. Mothering, for instance. Baking, I measured.

Mix that flour and salt in a bowl. I always used my largest, white with blue stripes round the side. A wedding gift from my mama, come in a nested set, three different sizes. Like him and his two brothers, Eamon liked to say. Then cut in a cup of Crisco with a pastry blender, it looks sort of like a small harp. When he was young and still in the kitchen, Eamon'd play on it a time or two, just to show me.

You got to work that fat in real good, blend it, all the way through. The recipes say "till it looks like small peas," but that ain't nowhere near enough. I pity the woman what tries to make piecrust from the recipe on the side of a tin of Crisco, I sure do. You got to mix it in completely. Stop too soon, all you got's lumps of fat with flour on the outside. Never get a piecrust out of that. Get it right, though, and it clumps up on its own. More you mix, the bigger they get. Pea-size ain't near enough, no sir. Needs to be lima beans. Bigger, even.

Then add your water, a tablespoon at a time. Mix well after each one. Four tablespoons in all, that's a quarter cup. Less sometimes, if it's real humid.

It was humid the day that Eamon left, ever'body's clothes sticking to 'em like a second skin.

Well.

Dust your hands with flour, make the dough into a ball. Knead it a bit if you like, just to be sure. And don't pay no never mind to them that says too much handling makes that pie crust tough. You don't got to worry about that at all, uh-uh. The more you handle it, the better.

Babies are like that, too. Folks think you spoil 'em, picking them up whenever they cry. But some babies need it. They just have to feel your hands on 'em. You can carry them around with you all day if you have to. No sir, if it's one thing I know, holding them close is the making of men, not the ruining.

Next, you gotta roll that dough out. Cut it in two. Plunk half on a piece of wax paper dusted with a little flour, soft as talc. Cover with more of that wax paper, a little flour'll keep that from sticking, too. A bottle of pop will do in a pinch if you don't have a rolling pin. Roll it thin, peel the top paper off, and take the bottom with the pie crust on it and flip it into a pie plate. Peel the paper off real careful-like, but don't pay no mind if it tears – just dip your fingers in some flour and press it right back. Mends up fine and no one'll ever know the difference.

But you can only compare a boy and a pie so far.

Put the filling in, roll the other crust out, too, and put that on top. Crimp the sides together real good so it don't leak none and cut some slits on top, for the steam.

Bake it, four hundred-twenty-five degrees, forty-five minutes to an hour, depending what-all's inside.

Best pie I ever made? Oh, that was on an early summer day, like I said, more'n forty years ago now. Ain't never made another. Promised myself I wouldn't, not till he come back home.

Well.

I remember it like yesterday. All of us smiling and laughing, talking and talking about nothing really, no sir. Eamon was like a brand-new penny that day, shining, handsome, everything before him. Telling me how much he loved me and respected his daddy, the two of them clapping each other on the back every time they was in spitting distance. Eamon even said he loved his germy younger brothers, punching them in the shoulder all day long, and then hugging them tight, just the once. His daddy was so proud of him. Funny how a suit with brass buttons can make a man lose all sense.

"It's an honour to serve," Eamon said. And I knew what he meant, I surely did.

The whole family was there, uncles and aunts, cousins, friends and neighbours, too. Even the mayor, like it was some goddamn Fourth of July. We laid on a barbeque, just the way he liked it – ribs, cole slaw, potato salad, devilled eggs, corn on the cob, biscuits, watermelon, and of course his favourite, rhubarb pie. Made four of 'em that morning. Ever'body said I made the lightest crust around. Like I told you, the trick is to work it enough, to get everything mixed in just right.

Women often fail at pie because they give up too soon.

I brought it out to him, still warm from the oven, ice cream on the side. Eamon liked it that way, the tart bleeding into the sweet.

The light from the sun slanted long and low.

"If anything happens," he said.

And I hushed him, wouldn't hear it. Just wouldn't. I told him, "You finish that pie now, son. Your ice cream's melting in the heat."

WHAT I'VE PRAYED FOR

A dog. A pony. A bike. To pass the test. A good report card. To be popular; to be prettier; to be prettier than Rebecca. To win first prize. To make the bullying stop.

Better parents. My parents to be dead. A bra. My period. Breasts large enough to inspire interest. My parents to let me be. My parents to take an interest. Implants. A nose job. To get laid. A lock on my door. Answers. For the arguing to stop. For Mom to stop drinking. For Dad to quit hitting her. My parents to split up. My parents to get back together. To lose weight. To stop puking. Bigger breasts. A clear complexion.

A cure for the cold sore that's ruining my life.

To be like everyone else. To be unique. White teeth. Joel to look at me. Rob to talk to me. Jeff to ask me to the dance. Tak to take me to the prom. To top 1300 on my SATs. A motorcycle. Admission to the college of my choice. Admission to a second-tier college. Admission to college.

To get out of this damn college with the fucking degree.

RU-486. Bryan to stop calling me. Bryan to quit stalking me. Bryan to obey the restraining order. A career. A job. A minimum wage I can live on. A car. To pay off my student loan. Talent. Implants. Respect. Fame. Notoriety.

A Lexus.

A boyfriend. Another boyfriend. My period. An abortion. Smaller thighs; better conversation. A good job. A promotion. A job. To fall in love.

For Paul to stop playing the field. For Paul to move in with me. For Paul to propose. A big wedding. Our own home. A baby. A baby. A baby. To conceive. To not have to fuck by the calendar.

To stop puking. Natural childbirth. An epidural. A C-section. Morphine. Morphine. MORPHINE!

A full night's sleep, just one.

A house with four bedrooms, two bathrooms, and a master ensuite. More sleep. Another baby. Any sleep. Maternity leave. Daycare. A good babysitter. A babysitter. A babysitter who isn't a psycho.

My luck to change.

A winning lottery ticket.

Some way to return the money.

A family doctor. Broadband. A renovated kitchen: oak, granite, and stainless steel. Lower mortgage payments. More time from the bank. A good credit counselor.

Not to get caught.

A divorce. A better lawyer. Visitation rights.

A tummy tuck. A boyfriend. A new car. A cruise. My ship to come in.

Peace, order, and good government. Canada World Youth. Parents. The world. Disarmament. Peace in our time. Peace. Liberty and justice for all. To do the right thing. A pension. Grandchildren. A Florida condo. Clean air, clean water.

Air.

Water.

For my memory to… well, I know it was something to do with my memory.

The cure for loneliness.

The mammogram to be okay. The colonoscopy to be normal. That mole to be just a mole.

Remission.

Someone who'll visit.

Morphine.

Meaning.

Not to die first. Not to die alone. Not to

ABOUT THE AUTHOR

After over two decades in molecular genetics research, Beverly Akerman realized she'd been learning more and more about less and less. Skittish at the prospect of knowing everything about nothing, she turned, for solace, to writing. Her fiction has appeared in Canada, the USA, and Germany. Her recognitions include the David Adams Richards Prize; nominations for a Pushcart Prize and Best of the Web Award; an Editor's Choice Award, *Best New Writing 2011*/Hoffer Prize; a Fishtrap Fellowship; first prize, *The Vocabula Review* Well-Written Writing Contest, *Gemini Magazine's* Flash Fiction Contest, and Fog City Writers Short Story Contest; second place, Sheldon Currie Prize; honourable mention, *The Potomac Review* Fiction Prize, and *The Binnacle's* Ultra-Short Competition; finalist, *Freefall Magazine's* Prose Contest, TWUC's Short Prose Competition (twice), and for the Glass Woman Prize (twice). Her nonfiction has appeared in *Grain, The Hill Times, Maclean's, The Montreal Gazette, The National Post, Rampike, The Toronto Star*, on CBC Radio One's *Sunday Edition* and in many other lay and academic publications. Ms. Akerman lives in Montreal with her husband and three children. It pleases her strangely to believe she's the only Canadian fiction writer ever to have sequenced her own DNA.

ACKNOWLEDGEMENTS

Most of these stories have appeared (or are at press) in the following journals, some in slightly altered form: "Tumbalalaika" was originally published in *The Antigonish Review*; "Like Jeremy Irons" in *carte blanche*; "The Mysteries" in *The Dalhousie Review*; "Paternity" in *Descant*; "Sea of Tranquillity" in *Fog City Review* and *Best New Writing 2011*; "Pie" in *Gemini Magazine*; "Academic Freedom," "Pour Un Instant," and "The Woman with Deadly Hands" in *The Nashwaak Review*; "What I've Prayed For" in *The New Quarterly*; "Lighter Than Air" in *r.kv.r.y. quarterly*, and "Broken" in *Windsor Review*.

RECYCLED
Paper made from
recycled material
FSC® C005834
FSC
www.fsc.org